$5.56

* * * * * *

THE
WORLD
OUTSIDE

* * * * * * * * * * *

THE WORLD OUTSIDE

* * * * *

collected short fiction

about women

at work

* * * * *

selected by
ANN REIT

drawings by
LUCY MARTIN BITZER

* * *

FOUR WINDS PRESS   NEW YORK

FOR REPRINT PERMISSION, GRATEFUL ACKNOWLEDGMENT IS MADE TO:

Andre Deutsch Limited for British Commonwealth rights to "Mannequin" from TIGERS ARE BETTER LOOKING by Jean Rhys.

Doubleday & Company, Inc. for "The Trimmed Lamp" from THE TRIMMED LAMP by O. Henry, copyright 1907 by Doubleday & Company, Inc.

Harper & Row, Publishers, Inc. for "Mannequin" from TIGERS ARE BETTER LOOKING by Jean Rhys, 1974.

Houghton Mifflin Co. for "Martha's Lady" from THE COUNTRY OF THE POINTED FIRS by Sarah Orne Jewett.

Alfred A. Knopf, Inc. for "A Gold Slipper" from YOUTH AND THE BRIGHT MEDUSA by Willa Cather; "A Gourdful of Glory" from THE TOMORROW-TAMER by Margaret Laurence, copyright © 1960 by Margaret Laurence; and "The Singing Lesson" from THE SHORT STORIES OF KATHERINE MANSFIELD, copyright 1922 by Alfred A. Knopf, Inc. and renewed 1950 by John Middleton Murry.

Macmillan London and Basingstoke for British Commonwealth rights to "A Gourdful of Glory" from TOMORROW-TAMER by Margaret Laurence.

McClelland and Stewart, The Canadian Publishers, Toronto, for "A Gourdful of Glory" from TOMORROW-TAMER by Margaret Laurence.

McGraw-Hill Book Company, McGraw-Hill Ryerson, Canada, and Penguin Books Ltd. for "The Office" from DANCE OF THE HAPPY SHADES by Alice Munro, copyright © 1968 by Alice Munro.

Flora Roberts, Inc. for "The Pocketbook Game" from LIKE ONE OF THE FAMILY by Alice Childress, copyright © 1956 by Alice Childress.

* * * * * *

LIBRARY OF CONGRESS CATALOGING IN PUBLICATION DATA

Main entry under title:
The World outside.

CONTENTS: Jewett, S. O. Martha's lady.—Munro, A. The office.—Henry, O. The trimmed lamp.—Smith, J. W. Frankie Mae. [etc.]
1. Women—Employment—Juvenile fiction. 2. Short stories. [1. Women—Employment—Fiction. 2. Short stories] I. Reit, Ann.
PZ5.W826   [Fic]   77–7986
ISBN 0–590–07484–9
ISBN 0–590–01396–3 pbk.

PUBLISHED BY FOUR WINDS PRESS
A DIVISION OF SCHOLASTIC MAGAZINES, INC., NEW YORK, N.Y.
TEXT COPYRIGHT © 1977 BY ANN REIT
ILLUSTRATIONS COPYRIGHT © 1977 BY LUCY MARTIN BITZER
ALL RIGHTS RESERVED
PRINTED IN THE UNITED STATES OF AMERICA
LIBRARY OF CONGRESS CATALOG CARD NUMBER: 77–7986
1   2   3   4   5   81 80 79 78 77

* * * * * * * * * * *

For the women in my family,

here and gone

CONTENTS

INTRODUCTION

It is only recently that there has been any real inter-
est in the subject of working women. Because of this, many
people think that it is only in the twentieth century or the
post-Industrial-Revolution society that women have worked.
The truth is that women have always worked—there just
wasn't much attention paid to this fact.

Sappho was writing some of the best Greek lyric poetry in
the early sixth century B.C. Muraski Shikibu wrote one of
the first great works of fiction in Japanese in the eleventh
century. Artemisia Gentileschi was painting in Italy in the
early 1600s and Élisabeth Vigée-Lebrun in France in the
late 1700s. Elizabeth I was a hardworking queen in 1558.

In America, Margaret Brent was a lawyer in Maryland in
1642. Mary Katherine Goddard was authorized to print the
official copy of the Declaration of Independence for state
legislatures in 1777, and her mother, Sarah Updike Goddard,
was publisher of the *Providence Gazette*. Sarah Alock was a
doctor in Massachusetts in the mid 1600s. Who worked
harder than the nineteenth-century feminists or the labor
agitator Mother Jones? In the period in which *we* are living,
nine out of ten women in America will work at some time
during their lives.

All the stories in this collection are about women who
work. They are about how women use their work, how it
affects them, and how other people relate to it. The kind of
work they do is secondary to the attitudes that are expressed.

Martha in "Martha's Lady" and Miss Meadows in "The
Singing Lesson" are totally different women. Martha, at the
beginning of the story, is clumsy, slow and confused; Miss
Meadows is an educated woman. Yet Martha, as the years
go by, becomes an expert at her work; her work becomes
an expression of her innate good taste. Miss Meadows, however, uses her work badly. When she is happy, she is a loving
teacher; when she is unhappy, she is a tyrant.

In "The Tone of Time," Mary Tredwick works in bitter-
ness; Mildred in "The Pocketbook Game" works with humor;
Mammii Ama in "A Gourdful of Glory" works with pride.
Frankie Mae is destroyed by the work she is forced to do;
Nancy in "The Trimmed Lamp" tries to use her work to
expand her life.

Esther Kahn works to please a man; Clementina Knox
in "Echo from Ithaca" works in spite of a man; the writer
in "The Office" finds her work is disrupted by a man. Kitty
Ayrshire in "The Gold Slipper" has an almost intellectual
approach to work; the mannequin's is physical.

All the protagonists in the stories are women, and all work.
They are very different women in their personalities, circumstances, and needs. But in every case the work the woman
does is the loom on which the story is woven.

Larger areas of work are now becoming available to
women, and women can now allow themselves to be ambitious and assertive in the same ways men have been. This
is a time when more women are seeing their work as ex-
pressions of important aspects of themselves. More women
are learning to enjoy the creativeness, supportiveness, and
happiness that work can afford. For while human relation-
ships may vary and change through the years, work can be
a continuing and constant part of a woman's life.

MARTHA'S LADY

* * * * * * * *

* * * * *

by Sarah Orne Jewett

*O*ne day, many years ago, the old Judge Pyne house wore an unwonted look of gayety and youthfulness. The high-fenced green garden was bright with June flowers. Under the elms in the large shady front yard you might see some chairs placed near together, as they often used to be when the family were all at home and life was going on gayly with eager talk and pleasure-making; when the elder judge, the grandfather, used to quote that great author, Dr. Johnson, and say to his girls, "Be brisk, be splendid, and be public."

One of the chairs had a crimson silk shawl thrown carelessly over its straight back, and a passer-by, who looked in through the latticed gate between the tall gate-posts with their white urns, might think that this piece of shining East Indian color was a huge red lily that had suddenly bloomed against the syringa bush. There were certain windows thrown wide open that were usually shut, and their curtains were blowing free in the light wind of a summer afternoon; it looked as if a large household had returned to the old house to fill the prim best rooms and find them full of cheer.

It was evident to everyone in town that Miss Harriet Pyne, to use the village phrase, had company. She was the last of her family, and was by no means old; but being the last, and wonted to live with people much older than herself, she had formed all the habits of a serious elderly person.

Ladies of her age, something past thirty, often wore discreet
caps in those days, especially if they were married, but
being single, Miss Harriet clung to youth in this respect,
making the one concession of keeping her waving chestnut
hair as smooth and stiffly arranged as possible. She had been
the dutiful companion of her father and mother in their
latest years, all her elder brothers and sisters having married
and gone, or died and gone, out of the old house. Now that
she was left alone it seemed quite the best thing frankly to
accept the fact of age, and to turn more resolutely than ever
to the companionship of duty and serious books. She was
more serious and given to routine than her elders themselves,
as sometimes happened when the daughters of New England
gentlefolks were brought up wholly in the society of their
elders. At thirty-five she had more reluctance than her
mother to face an unforeseen occasion, certainly more than
her grandmother, who had preserved some cheerful in-
heritance of gayety and worldliness from colonial times.

There was something about the look of the crimson silk
shawl in the front yard to make one suspect that the sober
customs of the best house in a quiet New England village
were all being set at defiance, and once when the mistress
of the house came to stand in her own doorway, she wore
the pleased but somewhat apprehensive look of a guest. In
these days New England life held the necessity of much
dignity and discretion of behavior; there was the truest
hospitality and good cheer in all occasional festivities, but
it was sometimes a self-conscious hospitality, followed by
an inexorable return to asceticism both of diet and of
behavior. Miss Harriet Pyne belonged to the very dullest
days of New England, those which perhaps held the most

priggishness for the learned professions, the most limited
interpretation of the word "evangelical," and the pettiest
indifference to large things. The outbreak of a desire for
larger religious freedom caused at first a most determined
reaction toward formalism, especially in small and quiet
villages like Ashford, intently busy with their own concerns.
It was high time for a little leaven to begin its work, in
this moment when the great impulses of the war for liberty
had died away and those of the coming war for patriotism
and a new freedom had hardly yet begun.

The dull interior, the changed life of the old house, whose
former activities seemed to have fallen sound asleep, really
typified these larger conditions, and a little leaven had
made its easily recognized appearance in the shape of a
light-hearted girl. She was Miss Harriet's young Boston
cousin, Helena Vernon, who, half-amused and half-impa-
tient at the unnecessary sober-mindedness of her hostess
and of Ashford in general, had set herself to the difficult
task of gayety. Cousin Harriet looked on at a succession
of ingenious and, on the whole, innocent attempts at pleasure,
as she might have looked on at the frolics of a kitten who
easily substitutes a ball of yarn for the uncertainties of a
bird or a wind-blown leaf, and who may at any moment
ravel the fringe of a sacred curtain-tassle in preference to
either.

Helena, with her mischievous appealing eyes, with her
enchanting old songs and her guitar, seemed the more delightful and even reasonable because she was so kind to
everybody, and because she was a beauty. She had the gift
of most charming manners. There was all the unconscious

lovely ease and grace that had come with the good breeding of her city home, where many pleasant people came and went; she had no fear, one had almost said no respect, of the individual, and she did not need to think of herself. Cousin Harriet turned cold with apprehension when she saw the minister coming in at the front gate, and wondered in agony if Martha were properly attired to go to the door, and would by any chance hear the knocker; it was Helena who, delighted to have anything happen, ran to the door to welcome the Reverend Mr. Crofton as if he were a congenial friend of her own age. She could behave with more or less propriety during the stately first visit, and even contrive to lighten it with modest mirth, and to extort the confession that the guest had a tenor voice, though sadly out of practice; but when the minister departed a little flattered, and hoping that he had not expressed himself too strongly for a pastor upon the poems of Emerson, and feeling the unusual stir of gallantry in his proper heart, it was Helena who caught the honored hat of the late Judge Pyne from its last resting-place in the hall, and holding it securely in both hands, mimicked the minister's self-conscious entrance. She copied his pompous and anxious expression in the dim parlor in such delicious fashion that Miss Harriet, who could not always extinguish a ready spark of the original sin of humor, laughed aloud.

"My dear!" she exclaimed severely the next moment, "I am ashamed of your being so disrespectful!" and then laughed again, and took the affecting old hat and carried it back to its place.

"I would not have had any one else see you for the world," she said sorrowfully as she returned, feeling quite self-

* * * *

possessed again, to the parlor doorway; but Helena still
sat in the ministers' chair, with her small feet placed as his
stiff boots had been, and a copy of his solemn expression
before they came to speaking of Emerson and of the guitar.
"I wish I had asked him if he would be so kind as to climb
the cherry-tree," said Helena, unbending a little at the discovery that her cousin would consent to laugh no more.
"There are all those ripe cherries on the top branches. I can
climb as high as he, but I can't reach far enough from the
last branch that will bear me. The minister is so long and
thin"—

"I don't know what Mr. Crofton would have thought of
you; he is a very serious young man," said cousin Harriet,
still ashamed of her laughter. "Martha will get the cherries
for you, or one of the men. I should not like to have Mr.
Crofton think you were frivolous, a young lady of your opportunities"—but Helena had escaped through the hall
and out at the garden door at the mention of Martha's name.
Miss Harriet Pyne sighed anxiously, and then smiled, in
spite of her deep convictions, as she shut the blinds and tried
to make the house look solemn again.

The front door might be shut, but the garden door at
the other end of the broad hall was wide open upon the
large sunshiny garden, where the last of the red and white
peonies and the golden lilies, and the first of the tall blue
larkspurs lent their colors in generous fashion. The straight
box borders were all in fresh and shining green of their
new leaves, and there was a fragrance of the old garden in-
most life and soul blowing from the honeysuckle blossoms
on a long trellis. It was now late in the afternoon, and the
sun was low behind great apple-trees at the garden's end,

which threw their shadows over the short turf of the bleaching-green. The cherry-trees stood at one side in full sunshine,
and Miss Harriet, who presently came to the garden steps to
watch like a hen at the water's edge, saw her cousin's pretty
figure in its white dress of India muslin hurrying across
the grass. She was accompanied by the tall, ungainly shape
of Martha the new maid, who, dull and indifferent to every
one else, showed a surprising willingness and allegiance to
the young guest.

"Martha ought to be in the dining-room, already, slow
as she is; it wants but half an hour of tea-time," said Miss
Harriet, as she turned and went into the shaded house. It
was Martha's duty to wait at table, and there had been
many trying scenes and defeated efforts toward her education. Martha was certainly very clumsy, and she seemed the
clumsier because she had replaced her aunt, a most skillful
person, who had but lately married a thriving farm and its
prosperous owner. It must be confessed that Miss Harriet
was a most bewildering instructor, and that her pupil's
brain was easily confused and prone to blunders. The coming of Helena had been somewhat dreaded by reason of
this incompetent service, but the guest took no notice of
frowns or futile gestures at the first tea-table, except to
establish friendly relations with Martha on her own account
by a reassuring smile. They were about the same age, and
next morning, before cousin Harriet came down, Helena
showed by a word and a quick touch the right way to do
something that had gone wrong and been impossible to
understand the night before. A moment later the anxious
mistress came in without suspicion, but Martha's eyes were
as affectionate as a dog's, and there was a new look of hope-

fulness on her face; this dreaded guest was a friend after all, and not a foe come from proud Boston to confound her ignorance and patient efforts.

The two young creatures, mistress and maid, were hurrying across the bleaching-green.

"I can't reach the ripest cherries," explained Helena politely, "and I think that Miss Pyne ought to send some to the minister. He has just made us a call. Why, Martha, you haven't been crying again!"

"Yes'm," said Martha sadly. "Miss Pyne always loves to send something to the minister," she acknowledged with interest, as if she did not wish to be asked to explain these latest tears.

"We'll arrange some of the best cherries in a pretty dish. I'll show you how, and you shall carry them over to the parsonage after tea," said Helena cheerfully, and Martha accepted the embassy with pleasure. Life was beginning to hold moments of something like delight in the last few days.

"You'll spoil your pretty dress, Miss Helena," Martha gave shy warning, and Miss Helena stood back and held up her skirts with unusual care while the country girl, in her heavy blue checked gingham, began to climb the cherry-tree like a boy.

Down came the scarlet fruit like bright rain into the green grass.

"Break some nice twigs with the cherries and leaves together; oh, you're a duck, Martha!" and Martha, flushed with delight, and looking far more like a thin and solemn blue heron, came rustling down to earth again, and gathered the spoils into her clean apron.

That night at tea, during her handmaiden's temporary

absence. Miss Harriet announced, as if by way of apology, that she thought Martha was beginning to understand something about her work. "Her aunt was a treasure, she never had to be told anything twice; but Martha has been as clumsy as a calf," said the precise mistress of the house. "I have been afraid sometimes that I never could teach her anything. I was quite ashamed to have you come just now, and find me so unprepared to entertain a visitor."

"Oh, Martha will learn fast enough because she cares so much," said the visitor eagerly. "I think she is a dear good girl. I do hope that she will never go away. I think she does things better every day, cousin Harriet," added Helena pleadingly, with all her kind young heart. The china-closet door was open a little way, and Martha heard every word. From that moment, she not only knew what love was like; but she knew love's dear ambitions. To have come from a stony hill-farm and a bare small wooden house, was like a cave-dweller's coming to make a permanent home in an art museum, such had seemed the elaborateness and elegance of Miss Pyne's fashion of life; and Martha's simple brain was slow enough in its processes and recognitions. But with this sympathetic ally and defender, this exquisite Miss Helena who believed in her, all difficulties appeared to vanish.

Later that evening, no longer homesick or hopeless, Martha returned from her polite errand to the minister, and stood with a sort of triumph before the two ladies, who were sitting in the front doorway, as if they were waiting for visitors, Helena still in her white muslin and red ribbons, and Miss Harriet in a thin black silk. Being happily self-forgetful in the greatness of the moment, Martha's manners were perfect, and she looked for once almost pretty and quite as young as she was.

"The minister came to the door himself, and returned his thanks. He said that cherries were always his favorite fruit, and he was much obliged to both Miss Pyne and Miss Vernon. He kept me waiting a few minutes, while he got this book ready to send to you, Miss Helena."

"What are you saying, Martha? I have sent him nothing!" exclaimed Miss Pyne, much astonished. "What does she mean, Helena?"

"Only a few cherries," explained Helena. "I thought Mr. Crofton would like them after his afternoon of parish calls. Martha and I arranged them before tea, and I sent them with our compliments."

"Oh, I am very glad you did," said Miss Harriet, wondering, but much relieved. "I was afraid"—

"No it was none of my mischief," answered Helena daringly. "I did not think that Martha would be ready to go so soon. I should have shown you how pretty they looked among their green leaves. We put them in one of your best white dishes with the openwork edge. Martha shall show you to-morrow; mamma always likes to have them so." Helena's fingers were busy with the hard knot of a parcel.

"See this, cousin Harriet!" she annnounced proudly, as Martha disappeared round the corner of the house, beaming with the pleasures of adventure and success. "Look! the minister has sent me a book: Sermons on *what?* Sermons— it is so dark that I can't quite see."

"It must be his 'Sermons on the Seriousness of Life'; they are the only ones he has printed, I believe," said Miss Harriet, with much pleasure. "They are considered very fine discourses. He pays you a great compliment, my dear. I feared that he noticed your girlish levity."

"I behaved beautifully while he stayed," insisted Helena. "Ministers are only men," but she blushed with pleasure. It was certainly something to receive a book from its author, and such a tribute made her of more value to the whole reverent household. The minister was not only a man, but a bachelor, and Helena was at the age that best loves conquest; it was at any rate comfortable to be reinstated in cousin Harriet's good graces.

"Do ask the kind gentleman to tea! He needs a little cheering up," begged the siren in India muslin, as she laid the shiny black volume of sermons on the stone doorstep with an air of approval, but as if they had quite finished their mission.

"Perhaps I shall, if Martha improves as much as she has within the last day or two," Miss Harriet promised hopefully. "It is something I always dread a little when I am all alone, but I think Mr. Crofton likes to come. He converses so elegantly."

TWO

These were the days of long visits, before affectionate friends thought it quite worth while to take a hundred miles' journey merely to dine or to pass a night in one another's houses. Helena lingered through the pleasant weeks of early summer, and departed unwillingly at last to join

* * * *

her family at the White Hills, where they had gone, like other households of high social station, to pass the month of August out of town. The happy-hearted young guest left many lamenting friends behind her, and promised each that she would come back again next year. She left the minister a rejected lover, as well as the preceptor of the academy, but with their pride unwounded, and it may have been with wider outlooks upon the world and a less narrow sympathy both for their own work in life and for their neighbors' work and hindrances. Even Miss Harriet Pyne herself had lost some of the unnecessary provincialism and prejudice which had begun to harden a naturally good and open mind and affectionate heart. She was conscious of feeling younger and more free, and not so lonely. Nobody had ever been so gay, so fascinating, or so kind as Helena, so full of social resource, so simple and undemanding in her friendliness. The light of her young life cast no shadow on either young or old companions, her pretty clothes never seemed to make other girls look dull or out of fashion. When she went away up the street in Miss Harriet's carriage to take the slow train toward Boston and the gayeties of the new Profile House, where her mother waited impatiently with a group of Southern friends, it seemed as if there would never be any more picnics or parties in Ashford, and as if society had nothing left to do but to grow old and get ready for winter.

Martha came into Miss Helena's bedroom that last morning, and it was easy to see that she had been crying; she looked just as she did in that first sad week of homesickness and despair. All for love's sake she had been learning to do many

things, and to do them exactly right; her eyes had grown
quick to see the smallest chance for personal service. Nobody
could be more humble and devoted; she looked years older
than Helena, and wore already a touching air of caretaking.

"You spoil me, you dear Martha!" said Helena from the
bed. "I don't know what they will say at home, I am so
spoiled."

Martha went on opening the blinds to let in the brightness
of the summer morning, but she did not speak.

"You are getting on splendidly, aren't you?" continued
the little mistress. "You have tried so hard that you make
me ashamed of myself. At first you crammed all the flowers
together, and now you make them look beautiful. Last night
cousin Harriet was so pleased when the table was so
charming, and I told her that you did everything yourself,
every bit. Won't you keep the flowers fresh and pretty in
the house until I come back? It's so much pleasanter for
Miss Pyne, and you'll feed my little sparrows, won't you?
They're growing so tame."

"Oh, yes, Miss Helena!" and Martha looked almost angry
for a moment, then she burst into tears and covered her
face with her apron. "I couldn't understand a single thing
when I first came. I never had been anywhere to see anything, and Miss Pyne frightened me when she talked. It
was you made me think I could ever learn. I wanted to
keep the place, 'count of mother and the little boys; we're
dreadful hard pushed. Hepsy has been good in the kitchen;
she said she ought to have patience with me, for she was
awkward herself when she first came."

Helena laughed; she looked so pretty under the tasseled
white curtains.

"I dare say Hepsy tells the truth," she said. "I wish you
had told me about your mother. When I come again, some
day we'll drive up country, as you call it, to see her. Martha!
I wish you would think of me sometimes after I go away.
Won't you promise?" and the bright young face suddenly
grew grave. "I have hard times myself; I don't always learn
things that I ought to learn, I don't always put things
straight. I wish you wouldn't forget me ever, and would
just believe in me. I think it does help more than anything."

"I won't forget," said Martha slowly. "I shall think of
you every day." She spoke almost with indifference, as if
she had been asked to dust a room, but she turned aside
quickly and pulled the little mat under the hot water jug
quite out of its former straightness; then she hastened away
down the long white entry, weeping as she went.

THREE

To lose out of sight the friend whom one has loved and
lived to please is to lose joy out of life. But if love is true,
there comes presently a higher joy of pleasing the ideal, that
is to say, the perfect friend. The same old happiness is
lifted to a higher level. As for Martha, the girl who stayed
behind in Ashford, nobody's life could seem duller to those
who could not understand; she was slow of step, and her
eyes were almost always downcast as if intent upon inces-
sant toil; but they startled you when she looked up, with
their shining light. She was capable of the happiness of

holding fast to a great sentiment, the ineffable satisfaction
of trying to please one whom she truly loved. She never
thought of trying to make other people pleased with herself; all she lived for was to do the best she could for others,
and to conform to an ideal, which grew at last to be like a
saint's vision, a heavenly figure painted upon the sky.

On Sunday afternoons in summer, Martha sat by the window of her chamber, a low-storied little room, which looked
into the side yard and the great branches of an elm-tree.
She never sat in the old wooden rocking-chair except on
Sundays like this; it belonged to the day of rest and to
happy meditation. She wore her plain black dress and a
clean white apron, and held in her lap a little wooden box,
with a brass ring on top for a handle. She was past sixty
years of age and looked even older, but there was the same
look on her face that it had sometimes worn in girlhood.
She was the same Martha; her hands were old-looking and
work-worn, but her face still shone. It seemed like yesterday that Helena Vernon had gone away, and it was more
than forty years.

War and peace had brought their changes and great
anxieties, the face of the earth was furrowed by floods and
fire, the faces of mistress and maid were furrowed by smiles
and tears, and in the sky the stars shone on as if nothing
had happened. The village of Ashford added a few pages
to its unexciting history, the minister preached, the people
listened; now and then a funeral crept along the street, and
now and then the bright face of a little child rose above
the horizon of a family pew. Miss Harriet Pyne lived on in
the large white house, which gained more and more dis-

* * * *

tinction because it suffered no changes, save successive re-paintings and a new railing about its stately roof. Miss Harriet herself had moved far beyond the uncertainties of an anxious youth. She had long ago made all her decisions, and settled all necessary questions; her scheme of life was as faultless as the miniature landscape of a Japanese garden, and as easily kept in order. The only important change she would ever be capable of making was the final change to another and a better world; and for that nature itself would gently provide, and her own innocent life.

Hardly any great social event had ruffled the easy current of life since Helena Vernon's marriage. To this Miss Pyne had gone, stately in appearance and carrying gifts of some old family silver which bore the Vernon crest, but not without some protest in her heart against the uncertainties of married life. Helena was so equal to a happy independence and even to the assistance of other lives grown strangely dependent upon her quick sympathies and instinctive decisions, that it was hard to let her sink her personality in the affairs of another. Yet a brilliant English match was not without its attractions to an old-fashioned gentlewoman like Miss Pyne, and Helena herself was amazingly happy; one day there had come a letter to Ashford, in which her very heart seemed to beat with love and self-forgetfulness, to tell cousin Harriet of such new happiness and high hope. "Tell Martha all that I say about my dear Jack," wrote the eager girl; "please show my letter to Martha, and tell her that I shall come home next summer and bring the hand-somest and best man in the world to Ashford. I have told him all about the dear house and the dear garden; there never was such a lad to reach for cherries with his six-foot-two."

Miss Pyne, wondering a little, gave the letter to Martha, who took it deliberately and as if she wondered too, and went away to read it slowly by herself. Martha cried over it, and felt a strange sense of loss and pain; it hurt her heart a little to read about the cherry-picking. Her idol seemed to be less her own since she had become the idol of a stranger. She never had taken such a letter in her hands before, but love at last prevailed, since Miss Helena was happy, and she kissed the last page where her name was written, feeling over-bold, and laid the envelope on Miss Pyne's secretary without a word.

The most generous love cannot but long for reassurance, and Martha had the joy of being remembered. She was not forgotten when the day of the wedding drew near, but she never knew that Miss Helena had asked if cousin Harriet would not bring Martha to town, she should like to have Martha there to see her married. "She would help about the flowers," wrote the happy girl; "I know she will like to come, and I'll ask mamma to plan to have some one take her all about Boston and make her have a pleasant time after the hurry of the great day is over."

Cousin Harriet thought it was very kind and exactly like Helena, but Martha would be out of her element; it was most imprudent and girlish to have thought of such a thing. Helena's mother would be far from wishing for any unnecessary guest just then, in the busiest part of her household, and it was best not to speak of the invitation. Some day Martha should go to Boston if she did well, but not now. Helena did not forget to ask if Martha had come, and was astonished by the indifference of the answer. It was the first thing which reminded her that she was not a fairy prin-

* * * *

cess having everything her own way in that last day before
the wedding. She knew that Martha would have loved to be
near, for she could not help understanding in that moment
of her own happiness the love that was hidden in another
heart. Next day this happy young princess, the bride, cut
a piece of a great cake and put it into a pretty box that had
held one of her wedding presents. With eager voices calling
her, and all her friends about her, and her mother's face
growing more and more wistful at the thought of parting,
she still lingered and ran to take one or two trifles from her
dressing-table, a little mirror and some tiny scissors that
Martha would remember, and one of the pretty handkerchiefs marked with her maiden name. These she put in
the box too; it was half a girlish freak and fancy, but she
could not help trying to share her happiness, and Martha's
life was so plain and dull. She whispered a message, and
put the little package into cousin Harriet's hand for Martha
as she said good-by. She was very fond of cousin Harriet.
She smiled with a gleam of her old fun; Martha's puzzled
look and tall awkward figure seemed to stand suddenly before her eyes, as she promised to come again to Ashford.
Impatient voices called to Helena, her lover was at the
door, and she hurried away, leaving her old home and her
girlhood gladly. If she had only known it, as she kissed
cousin Harriet good-by, they were never going to see each
other again until they were old women. The first step that
she took out of her father's house that day, married, and
full of hope and joy, was a step that led her away from
the green elms of Boston Common and away from her own
country and those she loved best, to a brilliant, much-varied
foreign life, and to nearly all the sorrows and nearly all the
joys that the heart of one woman could hold or know.

* * * *

On Sunday afternoons Martha used to sit by the window in Ashford and hold the wooden box which a favorite young brother, who afterward died at sea, had made for her, and she used to take out of it the pretty little box with a gilded cover that had held the piece of wedding-cake, and the small scissors, and the blurred bit of a mirror in its silver case; as for the handkerchief with the narrow lace edge, once in two or three years she sprinkled it as if it were a flower, and spread it out in the sun on the old bleaching-green, and sat near by in the shrubbery to watch lest some bold robin or cherry-bird should seize it and fly away.

FOUR

Miss Harriet Pyne was often congratulated upon the good fortune of having such a helper and friend as Martha. As time went on this tall, gaunt woman, always thin, always slow, gained a dignity of behavior and simple affectionateness of look which suited the charm and dignity of the ancient house. She was unconsciously beautiful like a saint, like the picturesqueness of a lonely tree which lives to shelter unnumbered lives and to stand quietly in its place. There was such rustic homeliness and constancy belonging to her, such beautiful powers of apprehension, such reticence, such gentleness for those who were troubled or sick; all these gifts and graces Martha hid in her heart. She never joined the church because she thought she was not good enough, but life was such a passion and happiness of service that it was impossible not to be devout, and she was always in her humble place on Sundays, in the back pew next the door. She had been educated by a remembrance; Helena's young eyes forever looked at her reassuringly from a gay girlish face. Helena's sweet patience in teaching her own awkwardness could never be forgotten.

"I owe everything to Miss Helena," said Martha, half aloud, as she sat alone by the window; she had said it to herself a thousand times. When she looked in the little keepsake mirror she always hoped to see some faint reflection of Helena Vernon, but there was only her own brown old New England face to look back at her wonderingly.

Miss Pyne went less and less often to pay visits to her friends in Boston; there were very few friends left to come to Ashford and make long visits in the summer, and life grew more and more monotonous. Now and then there came news from across the sea and messages of remembrance, letters that were closely written on thin sheets of paper, and that spoke of lords and ladies, of great journeys, of the death of little children and the proud successes of boys at school, of the wedding of Helena Dysart's only daughter; but even that had happened years ago. These things seemed far away and vague, as if they belonged to a story and not to life itself; the true links with the past were quite different. There was the unvarying flock of ground-sparrows that Helena had begun to feed; every morning Martha scattered crumbs for them from the side doorsteps while Miss Pyne watched from the dining-room window, and they were counted and cherished year by year.

Miss Pyne herself had many fixed habits, but little ideality or imagination, and so at last it was Martha who took thought from her mistress, and gave freedom to her own good taste. After a while, without any one's observing the

change, the every-day ways of doing things in the house
came to be the stately ways that had once belonged only to
the entertainment of guests. Happily both mistress and
maid seized all possible chances for hospitality, yet Miss
Harriet nearly always sat alone at her exquisitely served
table with its fresh flowers, and the beautiful old china
which Martha handled so lovingly that there was no good
excuse for keeping it hidden on closet shelves. Every year
when the old cherry-trees were in fruit, Martha carried the
round white old English dish with a fretwork edge, full of
pointed green leaves and scarlet cherries, to the minister,
and his wife never quite understood why every year he
blushed and looked so conscious of the pleasure, and thanked
Martha as if he had received a very particular attention.
There was no pretty suggestion toward the pursuit of the
fine art of housekeeping in Martha's limited acquaintance
with newspapers that she did not adopt, there was no
refined old custom of the Pyne housekeeping that she consented to let go. And every day, as she had promised, she
thought of Miss Helena,—oh, many times in every day:
whether this thing would please her, or that be likely to
fall in with her fancy or ideas of fitness. As far as was
possible the rare news that reached Ashford through an
occasional letter or the talk of guests was made part of
Martha's own life, the history of her own heart. A worn old
geography often stood open at the map of Europe on the
lightstand in her room, and a little old-fashioned gilt button,
set with a bit of glass like a ruby, that had broken and
fallen from the trimming of one of Helena's dresses, was
used to mark the city of her dwelling-place. In the changes
of a diplomatic life Martha followed her lady all about
the map. Sometimes the button was at Paris, and some-

times at Madrid; once, to her great anxiety, it remained long at St. Petersburg. For such a slow scholar Martha was not unlearned at last, since everything about life in these foreign towns was of interest to her faithful heart. She satisfied her own mind as she threw crumbs to the tame sparrows; it was all part of the same thing and for the same affectionate reasons.

FIVE

One Sunday afternoon in early summer Miss Harriet Pyne came hurrying along the entry that led to Martha's room and called two or three times before its inhabitant could reach the door. Miss Harriet looked unusually cheerful and excited, and she held something in her hand. "Where are you, Martha?" she called again. "Come quick, I have something to tell you!"

"Here I am, Miss Pyne," said Martha, who had only stopped to put her precious box in the drawer, and to shut the geography.

"Who do you think is coming this very night at half-past six? We must have everything as nice as we can; I must see Hannah at once. Do you remember my cousin Helena who has lived abroad so long? Miss Helena Vernon,—the Honorable Mrs. Dysart, she is now."

"Yes, I remember her," answered Martha, turning a little pale.

"I knew that she was in this country, and I had written to ask her to come for a long visit," continued Miss Harriet,

who did not often explain things, even to Martha, though
she was always conscientious about the kind messages that
were sent back by grateful guests. "She telegraphs that she
means to anticipate her visit by a few days and come to
me at once. The heat is beginning in town, I suppose.
I daresay, having been a foreigner so long, she does not
mind traveling on Sunday. Do you think Hannah will be
prepared? We must have tea a little later."

"Yes, Miss Harriet," said Martha. She wondered that
she could speak as usual, there was such a ringing in her
ears. "I shall have time to pick some fresh strawberries;
Miss Helena is so fond of our strawberries."

"Why, I had forgotten," said Miss Pyne, a little puzzled
by something quite unusual in Martha's face. "We must
expect to find Mrs. Dysart a good deal changed, Martha; it
is a great many years since she was here; I have not seen
her since her wedding, and she has had a great deal of
trouble, poor girl. You had better open the parlor chamber,
and make it ready before you go down."

"It is all ready," said Martha. "I can carry some of those
little sweet-brier roses upstairs before she comes."

"Yes, you are always thoughtful," said Miss Pyne, with
unwonted feeling.

Martha did not answer. She glanced at the telegram wistfully. She had never really suspected before that Miss Pyne
knew nothing of the love that had been in her heart all
these years; it was half a pain and half a golden joy to keep
such a secret; she could hardly bear this moment of surprise.

Presently the news gave wings to her willing feet. When
Hannah, the cook, who never had known Miss Helena, went
to the parlor an hour later on some errand to her old mistress, she discovered that this stranger guest must be a very

* * * *

important person. She had never seen the tea-table look exactly as it did that night, and in the parlor itself there were fresh blossoming boughs in the old East India jars, and lilies in the paneled hall, and flowers everywhere, as if there were some high festivity.

Miss Pyne sat by the window watching in her best dress, looking stately and calm; she seldom went out now, and it was almost time for the carriage. Martha was just coming in from the garden with the strawberries, and with more flowers in her apron. It was a bright cool evening in June, the golden robins sang in the elms, and the sun was going down behind the apple-trees at the foot of the garden. The beautiful old house stood wide open to the long-expected guest.

"I think that I shall go down to the gate," said Miss Pyne, looking at Martha for approval, and Martha nodded and they went together slowly down the broad front walk.

There was a sound of horses and wheels on the roadside turf: Martha could not see at first; she stood back inside the gate behind the white lilac-bushes as the carriage came. Miss Pyne was there; she was holding out both arms and taking a tired, bent little figure in black to her heart. "Oh, my Miss Helena is an old woman like me!" and Martha gave a pitiful sob; she had never dreamed it would be like this; this was the one thing she could not bear.

"Where are you, Martha?" called Miss Pyne. "Martha will bring these in; you have not forgotten my good Martha, Helena?" Then Mrs. Dysart looked up and smiled just as she used to smile in the old days. The young eyes were there still in the changed face, and Miss Helena had come.

That night Martha waited in her lady's room just as she

used to, humble and silent, and went through with the old unforgotten loving services. The long years seemed like days. At last she lingered a moment trying to think of something else that might be done, then she was going silently away, but Helena called her back. She suddenly knew the whole story and could hardly speak.

"Oh, my dear Martha!" she cried, "won't you kiss me good-night? Oh, Martha, have you remembered like this, all these long years!"

THE OFFICE

* * * * * * * * *

* * * * *

by Alice Munro

*T*he solution to my life occurred to me one evening while I was ironing a shirt. It was simple but audacious. I went into the living room where my husband was watching television and I said, "I think I ought to have an office."

It sounded fantastic, even to me. What do I want an office for? I have a house; it is pleasant and roomy and has a view of the sea; it provides appropriate places for eating and sleeping, and having baths and conversations with one's friends. Also I have a garden; there is no lack of space.

No. But here comes the disclosure which is not easy for me: I am a writer. That does not sound right. Too presumptuous; phony, or at least unconvincing. Try again. I write. Is that better? I *try* to write. That makes it worse. Hypocritical humility. Well then?

It doesn't matter. However I put it, the words create their space of silence, the delicate moment of exposure. But people are kind, the silence is quickly absorbed by the solicitude of friendly voices, crying variously, how wonderful, and good for *you,* and well, that *is* intriguing. And what do you write, they inquire with spirit. Fiction, I reply, bearing my humiliation by this time with ease, even a suggestion of flippancy, which was not always mine, and again, again, the perceptible circles of dismay are smoothed out by such ready and tactful voices—which have however exhausted their stock of consolatory phrases, and can say only, *"Ah!"*

So this is what I want an office for (I said to my husband): to write in. I was at once aware that it sounded like
a finicky requirement, a piece of rare self-indulgence. To
write, as everyone knows, you need a typewriter, or at least
a pencil, some paper, a table and chair; I have all these
things in a corner of my bedroom. But now I want an office
as well.

And I was not even sure I was going to write in it,
if we come down to that. Maybe I would sit and stare at
the wall; even that prospect was not unpleasant to me. It
was really the sound of the word "office" that I liked, its
sound of dignity and peace. And purposefulness and importance. But I did not care to mention this to my husband, so I launched instead into a high-flown explanation
which went, as I remember, like this:

A house is all right for a man to work in. He brings his
work into the house, a place is cleared for it; the house
rearranges itself as best it can around him. Everybody
recognizes that his work *exists*. He is not expected to answer the telephone, to find things that are lost, to see why
the children are crying, or feed the cat. He can shut his
door. Imagine (I said) a mother shutting her door, and the
children knowing she is behind it; why, the very thought of
it is outrageous to them. A woman who sits staring into
space, into a country that is not her husband's or her
children's is likewise known to be an offence against nature.
So a house is not the same for a woman. She is not someone
who walks into the house, to make use of it, and will walk
out again. She *is* the house; there is no separation possible.

(And this is true, though as usual when arguing for some-

* * * *

thing I am afraid I do not deserve, I put it in too emphatic and emotional terms. At certain times, perhaps on long spring evenings, still rainy and sad, with the cold bulbs in bloom and a light too mild for promise drifting over the sea, I have opened the windows and felt the house shrink back into wood and plaster and those humble elements of which it is made, and the life in it subside, leaving me exposed, empty-handed, but feeling a fierce and lawless quiver of freedom, of loneliness too harsh and perfect for me now to bear. Then I know how the rest of the time I am sheltered and encumbered, how insistently I am warmed and bound.)

"Go ahead, if you can find one cheap enough," is all my husband had to say to this. He is not like me, he does not really want explanations. That the heart of another person is a closed book, is something you will hear him say frequently, and without regret.

Even then I did not think it was something that could be accomplished. Perhaps at bottom it seemed to me too improper a wish to be granted. I could almost more easily have wished for a mink coat, for a diamond necklace; these are things women do obtain. The children, learning of my plans, greeted them with the most dashing skepticism and unconcern. Nevertheless I went down to the shopping centre which is two blocks from where I live; there I had noticed for several months, and without thinking how they could pertain to me, a couple of For Rent signs in the upstairs windows of a building that housed a drugstore and a beauty parlour. As I went up the stairs I had a feeling of complete unreality; surely renting was a complicated business, in the case of offices; you did not simply knock on the

door of the vacant premises and wait to be admitted; it
would have to be done through channels. Also, they would
want too much money.

As it turned out, I did not even have to knock. A woman
came out of one of the empty offices, dragging a vacuum
cleaner, and pushing it with her foot, towards the open
door across the hall, which evidently led to an apartment in
the rear of the building. She and her husband lived in this
apartment; their name was Malley; and it was indeed they
who owned the building and rented out the offices. The
rooms she had just been vacuuming were, she told me,
fitted out for a dentist's office, and so would not interest
me, but she would show me the other place. She invited me
into her apartment while she put away the vacuum and got
her key. Her husband, she said with a sigh I could not
interpret, was not at home.

Mrs. Malley was a black-haired delicate-looking woman,
perhaps in her early forties, slatternly but still faintly
appealing, with such arbitrary touches of femininity as
the thin line of bright lipstick, the pink feather slippers
on obviously tender and swollen feet. She had the swaying
passivity, the air of exhaustion and muted apprehension,
that speaks of a life spent in close attention on a man who
is by turns vigorous, crotchety and dependent. How much
of this I saw at first, how much decided on later is of
course impossible to tell. But I did think that she would
have no children, the stress of her life, whatever it was, did
not allow it, and in this I was not mistaken.

The room where I waited was evidently a combination
living room and office. The first things I noticed were models
of ships—galleons, clippers, Queen Marys—sitting on the

tables, the window sills, the television. Where there were
no ships there were potted plants and a clutter of what are
sometimes called "masculine" ornaments—china deer heads,
bronze horses, huge ashtrays of heavy, veined, shiny material. On the walls were framed photographs and what
might have been diplomas. One photo showed a poodle
and a bulldog, dressed in masculine and feminine clothing,
and assuming with dismal embarrassment a pose of af-
fection. Written across it was "Old Friends." But the room
was really dominated by a portrait, with its own light and
a gilded frame; it was of a good-looking, fair-haired man
in middle age, sitting behind a desk, wearing a business
suit and looking preeminently prosperous, rosy and agreeable. Here again, it is probably hindsight on my part
that points out that in the portrait there is evident also some
uneasiness, some lack of faith the man has in this role,
a tendency he has to spread himself too bountifully and
insistently, which for all anyone knows may lead to disaster.

Never mind the Malleys. As soon as I saw that office, I
wanted it. It was larger than I needed, being divided in
such a way that it would be suitable for a doctor's office.
(We had a chiropractor in here but he left, says Mrs. Malley in her regretful but uninformative way.) The walls
were cold and bare, white with a little grey, to cut the glare
for the eyes. Since there were no doctors in evidence, nor
had been, as Mrs. Malley freely told me, for some time, I
offered twenty-five dollars a month. She said she would
have to speak to her husband.

The next time I came, my offer was agreed upon, and I
met Mr. Malley in the flesh. I explained, as I had already
done to his wife, that I did not want to make use of my
office during regular business hours, but during the week-

ends and sometimes in the evening. He asked me what I
would use it for, and I told him, not without wondering
first whether I ought to say I did stenography.

He absorbed the information with good humour. "Ah,
you're a writer."

"Well yes. I write."

"Then we'll do our best to see you're comfortable here,"
he said expansively. "I'm a great man for hobbies myself.
All these ship-models, I do them in my spare time, they're
a blessing for the nerves. People need an occupation for
their nerves. I daresay you're the same."

"Something the same," I said, resolutely agreeable, even
relieved that he saw my behaviour in this hazy and tolerant
light. At least he did not ask me, as I half-expected, who
was looking after the children, and did my husband approve? Ten years, maybe fifteen, had greatly softened,
spread and defeated the man in the picture. His hips and
thighs had now a startling accumulation of fat, causing him
to move with a sigh, a cushiony settling of flesh, a ponder-
ous matriarchal discomfort. His hair and eyes had faded,
his features blurred, and the affable, predatory expression
had collapsed into one troubling humility and chronic mis-
trust. I did not look at him. I had not planned, in taking
an office, to take on the responsibility of knowing any more
human beings.

On the weekend I moved in, without the help of my
family, who would have been kind. I brought my typewriter
and a card table and chair, also a little wooden table on
which I set a hot plate, a kettle, a jar of instant coffee, a
spoon and a yellow mug. That was all. I brooded with satisfaction on the bareness of my walls, the cheap dignity of

my essential furnishings, the remarkable lack of things to dust, wash or polish.

The sight was not so pleasing to Mr. Malley. He knocked on my door soon after I was settled and said that he wanted to explain a few things to me—about unscrewing the light in the outer room, which I would not need, about the radiator and how to work the awning outside the window. He looked around at everything with gloom and mystification and said it was an awfully uncomfortable place for a lady.

"It's perfectly all right for me," I said, not as discouragingly as I would have liked to, because I always have a tendency to placate people whom I dislike for no good reason, or simply do not want to know. I make elaborate offerings of courtesy sometimes, in the foolish hope that they will go away and leave me alone.

"What you want is a nice easy chair to sit in, while you're waiting for inspiration to hit. I've got a chair down in the basement, all kinds of stuff down there since my mother passed on last year. There's a bit of carpet rolled up in a corner down there, it isn't doing anybody any good. We could get this place fixed up so it'd be a lot more home-like for you."

But really, I said, but really I like it as it is.

"If you wanted to run up some curtains, I'd pay you for the material. Place needs a touch of colour, I'm afraid you'll get morbid sitting in here."

Oh, no, I said, and laughed, I'm sure I won't.

"It'd be a different story if you was a man. A woman wants things a bit cosier."

So I got up and went to the window and looked down into the empty Sunday street through the slats of the Venetian blind, to avoid the accusing vulnerability of his fat face and I tried out a cold voice that is to be heard frequently in my thoughts but has great difficulty getting out of my cowardly mouth. "Mr. Malley, please don't bother me about this any more. I said it suits me. I have everything I want. Thanks for showing me about the light."

The effect was devastating enough to shame me. "I certainly wouldn't dream of bothering you," he said, with precision of speech and aloof sadness. "I merely made these suggestions for your comfort. Had I realized I was in your way, I would of left some time ago." When he had gone I felt better, even a little exhilarated at my victory though still ashamed of how easy it had been. I told myself that he would have had to be discouraged sooner or later, it was better to have it over with at the beginning.

The following weekend he knocked on my door. His expression of humility was exaggerated, almost enough so to seem mocking, yet in another sense it was real and I felt unsure of myself.

"I won't take up a minute of your time," he said. "I never meant to be a nuisance. I just wanted to tell you I'm sorry I offended you last time and I apologize. Here's a little present if you will accept."

He was carrying a plant whose name I did not know; it had thick, glossy leaves and grew out of a pot wrapped lavishly in pink and silver foil.

"There," he said, arranging this plant in a corner of my room. "I don't want any bad feelings with you and me. I'll take the blame. And I thought, maybe she won't accept furnishings, but what's the matter with a nice little plant, that'll brighten things up for you."

It was not possible for me, at this moment, to tell him

that I did not want a plant. I hate house plants. He told me
how to take care of it, how often to water it and so on; I
thanked him. There was nothing else I could do, and I had
the unpleasant feeling that beneath his offering of apologies
and gifts he was well aware of this and in some way gratified by it. He kept on talking, using the words *bad feelings,
offended, apologize.* I tried once to interrupt, with the idea
of explaining that I had made provision for an area of my
life where good feelings, or bad, did not enter in, that between him and me, in fact, it was not necessary that there
be any feelings at all; but this struck me as a hopeless task.
How could I confront, in the open, this craving for intimacy?
Besides, the plant in its shiny paper had confused me.

"How's the writing progressing?" he said, with an air of
putting all our unfortunate differences behind him.

"Oh, about as usual."

"Well if you ever run out of things to write about, I got
a barrelful." Pause. "But I guess I'm just eatin' into your
time here," he said with a kind of painful buoyancy. This
was a test, and I did not pass it. I smiled, my eyes held by
that magnificent plant; I said it was all right.

"I was just thinking about the fellow was in here before
you. Chiropractor. You could of wrote a book about him."

I assumed a listening position, my hands no longer
hovering over the keys. If cowardice and insincerity are big
vices of mine, curiosity is certainly another.

"He had a good practice built up here. The only trouble
was, he gave more adjustments than was listed in the book
of chiropractory. Oh, he was adjusting right and left. I
came in here after he moved out, and what do you think I
found? Soundproofing! This whole room was soundproofed,

to enable him to make his adjustments without disturbing anybody. This very room you're sitting writing your stories in.

"First we knew of it was a lady knocked on my door one day, wanted me to provide her with a passkey to his office. He'd locked his door against her.

"I guess he just got tired of treating her particular case. I guess he figured he'd been knocking away at it long enough. Lady well on in years, you know, and him just a young man. He had a nice young wife too and a couple of the prettiest children you ever would want to see. Filthy some of the things that go on in this world."

It took me some time to realize that he told this story not simply as a piece of gossip, but as something a writer would be particularly interested to hear. Writing and lewdness had a vague delicious connection in his mind. Even this notion, however, seemed so wistful, so infantile, that it struck me as a waste of energy to attack it. I knew now I must avoid hurting him for my own sake, not for his. It had been a great mistake to think that a little roughness would settle things.

The next present was a teapot. I insisted that I drank only coffee and told him to give it to his wife. He said that tea was better for the nerves and that he had known right away I was a nervous person, like himself. The teapot was covered with a gilt and roses and I knew that it was not cheap, in spite of its extreme hideousness. I kept it on my table. I also continued to care for the plant, which thrived obscenely in the corner of my room. I could not decide what else to do. He bought me a wastebasket, a fancy one

with Chinese mandarins on all eight sides; he got a foam
rubber cushion for my chair. I despised myself for sub-
mitting to this blackmail. I did not even really pity him; it
was just that I could not turn away, I could not turn away
from that obsequious hunger. And he knew himself my tolerance was bought; in a way he must have hated me for it.

When he lingered in my office now he told me stories of
himself. It occurred to me that he was revealing his life to
me in the hope that I would write it down. Of course he
had probably revealed it to plenty of people for no particular reason, but in my case there seemed to be a special,
even desperate necessity. His life was a series of calamities,
as people's lives often are; he had been let down by people
he had trusted, refused help by those he had depended on,
betrayed by the very friends to whom he had given kindness and material help. Other people, mere strangers and
passersby, had taken time to torment him gratuitously,
in novel and inventive ways. On occasion, his very life had
been threatened. Moreover his wife was a difficulty, her
health being poor and her temperament unstable; what was
he to do? You see how it is, he said, lifting his hands, but I
live. He looked to me to say yes.

I took to coming up the stairs on tiptoe, trying to turn
my key without making a noise; this was foolish of course
because I could not muffle my typewriter. I actually considered writing in longhand, and wished repeatedly for the
evil chiropractor's soundproofing. I told my husband my
problem and he said it was not a problem at all. Tell him
you're busy, he said. As a matter of fact I did tell him; every
time he came to my door, always armed with a little gift
or an errand, he asked me how I was and I said that today

I was busy. Ah, then, he said, as he eased himself through
the door, he would not keep me a minute. And all the time,
as I have said, he knew what was going on in my mind,
how I weakly longed to be rid of him. He knew but could
not afford to care.

One evening after I had gone home I discovered that I
had left at the office a letter I had intended to post, and so
I went back to get it. I saw from the street that the light
was on in the room where I worked. Then I saw him bending over the card table. Of course, he came in at night and
read what I had written! He heard me at the door, and
when I came in he was picking up my wastebasket, saying
he thought he would just tidy things up for me. He went
out at once. I did not say anything, but found myself trembling with anger and gratification. To have found a just
cause was a wonder, an unbearable relief.

Next time he came to my door I had locked it on the inside. I knew his step, his chummy cajoling knock. I continued typing loudly, but not uninterruptedly, so he would
know I heard. He called my name, as if I was playing a
trick; I bit my lips together not to answer. Unreasonably as
ever, guilt assailed me but I typed on. That day I saw the
earth was dry around the roots of the plant; I let it alone.

I was not prepared for what happened next. I found a
note taped to my door, which said that Mr. Malley would
be obliged if I would step into his office. I went at once to
get it over with. He sat at his desk surrounded by obscure
evidences of his authority; he looked at me from a distance, as one who was now compelled to see me in a new
and sadly unfavourable light; the embarrassment which he

showed seemed not for himself, but me. He started off by saying, with a rather stagey reluctance, that he had known of course when he took me in that I was a writer.

"I didn't let that worry me, though I have heard things about writers and artists and that type of person that didn't strike me as very encouraging. You know the sort of thing I mean."

This was something new; I could not think what it might lead to.

"Now you came to me and said, Mr. Malley, I want a place to write in. I believed you. I gave it to you. I didn't ask any questions. That's the kind of person I am. But you know the more I think about it, well, the more I am inclined to wonder."

"Wonder what?" I said.

"And your own attitude, that hasn't helped to put my mind at ease. Locking yourself in and refusing to answer your door. That's not a normal way for a person to behave. Not if they got nothing to hide. No more than it's normal for a young woman, says she has a husband and kids, to spend her time rattling away on a typewriter."

"But I don't think that—"

He lifted his hand, a forgiving gesture. "Now all I ask is, that you be open and aboveboard with me. I think I deserve that much, and if you are using that office for any other purpose, or at any other times than you let on, and having your friends or whoever they are up to see you—"

"I don't know what you mean."

"And another thing, you claim to be a writer. Well I read quite a bit of material, and I never have seen your name in print. Now maybe you write under some other name?"

"No," I said.

"Well I don't doubt there are writers whose names I haven't heard," he said genially. "We'll let that pass. Just you give me your word of honour there won't be any more deceptions, or any carryings-on, et cetera, in that office you occupy—"

My anger was delayed somehow, blocked off by a stupid incredulity. I only knew enough to get up and walk down the hall, his voice trailing after me, and lock the door. I thought—I must go. But after I had sat down in my own room, my work in front of me, I thought again how much I liked this room, how well I worked in it, and I decided not to be forced out. After all, I felt, the struggle between us had reached a deadlock. I could refuse to open the door, refuse to look at his notes, refuse to speak to him when we met. My rent was paid in advance and if I left now it was unlikely that I would get any refund. I resolved not to care. I had been taking my manuscript home every night, to prevent his reading it, and now it seemed that even this precaution was beneath me. What did it matter if he read it, any more than if the mice scampered over it in the dark?

Several times after this I found notes on my door. I intended not to read them, but I always did. His accusations grew more specific. He had heard voices in my room. My behaviour was disturbing his wife when she tried to take her afternoon nap. (I never came in the afternoons, except on weekends.) He had found a whiskey bottle in the garbage.

I wondered a good deal about that chiropractor. It was not comfortable to see how the legends of Mr. Malley's life were built up.

As the notes grew more virulent our personal encounters ceased. Once or twice I saw his stooped, sweatered back

disappearing as I came into the hall. Gradually our relationship passed into something that was entirely fantasy.
He accused me now, by note, of being intimate with people
from *Numero Cinq*. This was a coffee-house in the neighbourhood, which I imagine he invoked for symbolic purposes. I felt that nothing much more would happen now,
the notes would go on, their contents becoming possibly
more grotesque and so less likely to affect me.

He knocked on my door on a Sunday morning, about
eleven o'clock. I had just come in and taken my coat off
and put my kettle on the hot plate.

This time it was another face, remote and transfigured,
that shone with the cold light of intense joy at discovering
the proofs of sin.

"I wonder," he said with emotion, "if you would mind
following me down the hall?"

I followed him. The light was on in the washroom. This
washroom was mine and no one else used it, but he had
not given me a key for it and it was always open. He
stopped in front of it, pushed back the door and stood with
his eyes cast down, expelling his breath discreetly.

"Now who done that?" he said, in a voice of pure sorrow.

The walls above the toilet and above the washbasin were
covered with drawings and comments of the sort you see
sometimes in public washrooms on the beach, and in town
hall lavatories in the little decaying towns where I grew up.
They were done with a lipstick, as they usually are. Someone must have got up here the night before, I thought,
possibly some of the gang who always loafed and cruised
around the shopping centre on Saturday nights.

"It should have been locked," I said, coolly and firmly as

if thus to remove myself from the scene. "It's quite a mess."

"It sure is. It's pretty filthy language, in my book. Maybe it's just a joke to your friends, but it isn't to me. Not to mention the art work. That's a nice thing to see when you open a door on your own premises in the morning."

I said, "I believe lipstick will wash off."

"I'm just glad I didn't have my wife see a thing like this. Upsets a woman that's had a nice bringing up. Now why don't you ask your friends up here to have a party with their pails and brushes? I'd like to have a look at the people with that kind of a sense of humour."

I turned to walk away and he turned heavily in front of me.

"I don't think there's any question how these decorations found their way onto my walls."

"If you're trying to say I had anything to do with it," I said, quite flatly and wearily, "you must be crazy."

"How did they get there then? Whose lavatory is this? Eh, whose?"

"There isn't any key to it. Anybody can come up here and walk in. Maybe some kids off the street came up here and did it last night after I went home, how do I know?"

"It's a shame the way the kids gets blamed for everything, when it's the elders that corrupts them. That's a thing you might do some thinking about, you know. There's laws. Obscenity laws. Applies to this sort of thing and literature too as I believe."

This is the first time I ever remember taking deep breaths, consciously, for purposes of self-control. I really wanted to murder him. I remember how soft and loathsome his face looked, with the eyes almost closed, nostrils extended to the soothing odour of righteousness, the odour of triumph. If this stupid thing had not happened, he would never have won. But he had. Perhaps he saw something in my face that unnerved him, even in this victorious moment, for he drew back to the wall, and began to say that actually, as a matter of fact, he had not really felt it was the sort of thing I personally would do, more the sort of thing that perhaps certain friends of mine—I got into my own room, shut the door.

The kettle was making a fearsome noise, having almost boiled dry. I snatched it off the hot plate, pulled out the plug and stood for a moment choking on rage. This spasm passed and I did what I had to do. I put my typewriter and paper on the chair and folded the card table. I screwed the top tightly on the instant coffee and put it and the yellow mug and the teaspoon into the bag in which I had brought them; it was still lying folded on the shelf. I wished childishly to take some vengeance on the potted plant, which sat in the corner with the flowery teapot, the wastebasket, the cushion, and—I forgot—a little plastic pencil sharpener behind it.

When I was taking things down to the car Mrs. Malley came. I had seen little of her since that first day. She did not seem upset, but practical and resigned.

"He is lying down," she said. "He is not himself."

She carried the bag with the coffee and the mug in it. She was so still I felt my anger leave me, to be replaced by an absorbing depression.

I have not yet found another office. I think that I will try again some day, but not yet. I have to wait at least until that picture fades that I see so clearly in my mind, though

I never saw it in reality—Mr. Malley with his rags and
brushes and a pail of soapy water, scrubbing in his clumsy
way, his deliberately clumsy way, at the toilet walls, stoop-
ing with difficulty, breathing sorrowfully, arranging in his
mind the bizarre but somehow never quite satisfactory nar-
rative of yet another betrayal of trust. While I arrange
words, and think it is my right to be rid of him.

THE TRIMMED LAMP

* * * * * * * *

* * * * *

by O. Henry

Of course there are two sides to the question. Let us look at the other. We often hear "shop-girls" spoken of. No such persons exist. There are girls who work in shops. They make their living that way. But why turn their occupation into an adjective? Let us be fair. We do not refer to the girls who live on Fifth Avenue as "marriage-girls."

Lou and Nancy were chums. They came to the big city to find work because there was not enough to eat at their homes to go around. Nancy was nineteen; Lou was twenty. Both were pretty, active country girls who had no ambition to go on the stage.

The little cherub that sits up aloft guided them to a cheap and respectable boarding-house. Both found positions and became wage-earners. They remained chums. It is at the end of six months that I would beg you to step forward and be introduced to them. Meddlesome Reader: My Lady Friends, Miss Nancy and Miss Lou. While you are shaking hands please take notice—cautiously—of their attire. Yes, cautiously; for they are as quick to resent a stare as a lady in a box at the horse show is.

Lou is a piece-work ironer in a hand laundry. She is clothed in a badly fitting purple dress, and her hat plume is four inches too long; but her ermine muff and scarf cost $25, and its fellow beasts will be ticketed in the windows at $7.98 before the season is over. Her cheeks are pink, and her light blue eyes bright. Contentment radiates from her.

Nancy you would call a shop-girl—because you have the

habit. There is no type; but a perverse generation is always seeking a type; so this is what the type should be. She has the high-ratted pompadour and the exaggerated straight-front. Her skirt is shoddy, but has the correct flare. No furs protect her against the bitter spring air, but she wears her short broadcloth jacket as jauntily as though it were Persian lamb! On her face and in her eyes, remorseless type-seeker, is the typical shop-girl expression. It is a look of silent but contemptuous revolt against cheated womanhood; of sad prophecy of the vengeance to come. When she laughs her loudest the look is still there. The same look can be seen in the eyes of Russian peasants; and those of us left will see it some day on Gabriel's face when he comes to blow us up. It is a look that should wither and abash man; but he has been known to smirk at it and offer flowers—with a string tied to them.

Now lift your hat and come away, while you receive Lou's cheery "See you again," and the sardonic, sweet smile of Nancy that seems, somehow, to miss you and go fluttering like a white moth up over the housetops to the stars.

The two waited on the corner for Dan. Dan was Lou's steady company. Faithful? Well, he was on hand when Mary would have had to hire a dozen subpœna servers to find her lamb.

"Ain't you cold, Nancy?" said Lou. "Say, what a chump you are for working in that old store for $8 a week! I made $18.50 last week. Of course ironing ain't as swell work as selling lace behind a counter, but it pays. None of us ironers make less than $10. And I don't know that it's any less respectful work, either."

"You can have it," said Nancy, with uplifted nose. "I'll take my eight a week and hall bedroom. I like to be among nice things and swell people. And look what a chance I've got! Why, one of our glove girls married a Pittsburgh—a steel maker, or blacksmith or something—the other day worth a million dollars. I'll catch a swell myself some time. I ain't bragging on my looks or anything; but I'll take my chances where there's big prizes offered. What show would a girl have in a laundry?"

"Why, that's where I met Dan," said Lou, triumphantly. "He came in for his Sunday shirt and collars and saw me at the first board, ironing. We all try to get to work at the first board. Ella Maginnis was sick that day, and I had her place. He said he noticed my arms first, how round and white they was. I had my sleeves rolled up. Some nice fellows come into laundries. You can tell 'em by their bringing their clothes in suit cases, and turning in the door sharp and sudden."

"How can you wear a waist like that, Lou?" said Nancy, gazing down at the offending article with sweet scorn in her heavy-lidded eyes. "It shows fierce taste."

"This waist?" said Lou, with wide-eyed indignation. "Why, I paid $16 for this waist. It's worth twenty-five. A woman left it to be laundered, and never called for it. The boss sold it to me. It's got yards and yards of hand embroidery on it. Better talk about that ugly, plain thing you've got on."

"This ugly, plain thing," said Nancy, calmly, "was copied from one that Mrs. Van Alstyne Fisher was wearing. The girls say her bill in the store last year was $12,000. I made mine, myself. It cost me $1.50. Ten feet away you couldn't tell it from hers."

"Oh, well," said Lou, good-naturedly, "if you want to starve and put on airs, go ahead. But I'll take my job and good wages; and after hours give me something as fancy and attractive to wear as I am able to buy."

But just then Dan came—a serious young man with a

ready-made necktie, who had escaped the city's brand of frivolity—an electrician earning $30 per week who looked upon Lou with the sad eyes of Romeo, and thought her embroidered waist a web in which any fly should delight to be caught.

"My friend, Mr. Owens—shake hands with Miss Danforth," said Lou.

"I'm mighty glad to know you, Miss Danforth," said Dan, with outstretched hand. "I've heard Lou speak of you so often."

"Thanks," said Nancy, touching his fingers with the tips of her cool ones, "I've heard her mention you—a few times."

Lou giggled.

"Did you get that handshake from Mrs. Van Alstyne Fisher, Nance?" she asked.

"If I did, you can feel safe in copying it," said Nancy.

"Oh, I couldn't use it at all. It's too stylish for me. It's intended to set off diamond rings, that high shake is. Wait till I get a few and then I'll try it."

"Learn it first," said Nancy, wisely, "and you'll be more likely to get the rings."

"Now, to settle this argument," said Dan, with his ready, cheerful smile, "let me make a proposition. As I can't take both of you up to Tiffany's and do the right thing, what do you say to a little vaudeville? I've got the tickets. How about looking at stage diamonds since we can't shake hands with the real sparklers?"

The faithful squire took his place close to the curb; Lou next, a little peacocky in her bright and pretty clothes; Nancy on the inside, slender, and soberly clothed as the sparrow, but with the true Van Alstyne Fisher walk—thus they set out for their evening's moderate diversion.

I do not suppose that many look upon a great department

store as an educational institution. But the one in which Nancy worked was something like that to her. She was surrounded by beautiful things that breathed of caste and refinement. If you live in an atmosphere of luxury, luxury is yours whether your money pays for it, or another's.

The people she served were mostly women whose dress, manners, and position in the social world were quoted as criterions. From them Nancy began to take toll—the best from each according to her view.

From one she would copy and practice a gesture, from another an eloquent lifting of an eyebrow, from others, a manner of walking, of carrying a purse, of smiling, of greeting a friend, of addressing "inferiors in station." From her best beloved model, Mrs. Van Alstyne Fisher, she made requisition for that excellent thing, a soft, low voice as clear as silver and as perfect in articulation as the notes of a thrush. Suffused in the aura of this high social refinement and good breeding, it was impossible for her to escape a deeper effect of it. As good habits are said to be better than good principles, so, perhaps, good manners are better than good habits. The teachings of your parents may not keep alive your New England conscience; but if you sit on a straight-back chair and repeat the words "prisms and pilgrims" forty times the devil will flee from you. And when Nancy spoke in the Van Alstyne Fisher tones she felt the thrill of *noblesse oblige* to her very bones.

There was another source of learning in the great departmental school. Whenever you see three or four shop-girls gather in a bunch and jingle their wire bracelets as an accompaniment to apparently frivolous conversation, do not think that they are there for the purpose of criticizing the way Ethel does her back hair. The meeting may lack the dignity of the deliberative bodies of man; but it has all the importance of the occasion on which Eve and her first daughter first put their heads together to make Adam understand his proper place in the household. It is Woman's Conference for Common Defense and Exchange of Strategical Theories of Attack and Repulse upon and against the World, which is a Stage, and Man, its Audience who Persists in Throwing Bouquets Thereupon. Woman, the most helpless of the young of any animal—with the fawn's grace but without its fleetness; with the bird's beauty but without its power of flight; with the honey-bee's burden of sweetness but without its—Oh, let's drop that simile—some of us may have been stung.

During this council of war they pass weapons one to another, and exchange stratagems that each has devised and formulated out of the tactics of life.

"I says to 'im," says Sadie, "ain't you the fresh thing! Who do you suppose I am, to be addressing such a remark to me? And what do you think he says to me?"

The heads, brown, black, flaxen, red, and yellow bob together; the answer is given; and the parry to the thrust is decided upon, to be used by each thereafter in passages-at-arms with the common enemy, man.

Thus Nancy learned the art of defense; and to women successful defense means victory.

The curriculum of a department store is a wide one. Perhaps no other college could have fitted her as well for her life's ambition—the drawing of a matrimonial prize.

Her station in the store was a favored one. The music room was near enough for her to hear and become familiar with the works of the best composers—at least to acquire the familiarity that passed for appreciation in the social world in which she was vaguely trying to set a tentative and aspiring foot. She absorbed the educating influence of art wares, of costly and dainty fabrics, of adornments that are almost culture to women.

The other girls soon became aware of Nancy's ambition. "Here comes your millionaire, Nancy," they would call to her whenever any man who looked the rôle approached her counter. It got to be a habit of men, who were hanging about while their women folk were shopping, to stroll over to the handkerchief counter and dawdle over the cambric squares. Nancy's imitation high-bred air and genuine dainty beauty was what attracted. Many men thus came to display their graces before her. Some of them may have been millionaires; others were certainly no more than their sedulous apes. Nancy learned to discriminate. There was a window at the end of the handkerchief counter; and she could see the rows of vehicles waiting for the shoppers in the street below. She looked and perceived that automobiles differ as well as do their owners.

Once a fascinating gentleman bought four dozen handkerchiefs, and wooed her across the counter with a King Cophetua air. When he had gone one of the girls said:

"What's wrong, Nance, that you didn't warm up to that fellow? He looks the swell article, all right, to me."

"Him?" said Nancy, with her coolest, sweetest, most impersonal, Van Alstyne Fisher smile; "not for mine. I saw him drive up outside. A 12 H.P. machine and an Irish chauffeur! And you saw what kind of handkerchiefs he bought —silk! And he's got dactylis on him. Give me the real thing or nothing, if you please."

Two of the most "refined" women in the store—a forelady and a cashier—had a few "swell gentlemen friends" with whom they now and then dined. Once they included Nancy in an invitation. The dinner took place in a spectacular café whose tables are engaged for New Year's Eve a year in advance. There were two "gentlemen friends"—one without any hair on his head—high living ungrew it; and we can prove it—the other a young man whose worth and sophistication he impressed upon you in two convincing ways—he swore that all the wine was corked; and he wore diamond cuff buttons. This young man perceived irresistible excellencies in Nancy. His taste ran to shop-girls; and here was one that added the voice and manners of his high social world to the franker charms of her own caste. So, on the following day, he appeared in the store and made her a serious proposal of marriage over a box of hemstitched, grass-bleached Irish linens. Nancy declined. A brown pompadour ten feet away had been using her eyes and ears. When the rejected suitor had gone she heaped carboys of upbraidings and horror upon Nancy's head.

"What a terrible little fool you are! That fellow's a millionaire—he's a nephew of old Van Skittles himself. And he was talking on the level, too. Have you gone crazy, Nance?"

"Have I?" said Nancy. "I didn't take him, did I? He isn't a millionaire so hard that you could notice it, anyhow. His family only allows him $20,000 a year to spend. The bald-headed fellow was guying him about it the other night at supper."

The brown pompadour came near and narrowed her eyes.

"Say, what do you want?" she inquired, in a voice hoarse for lack of chewing-gum. "Aint that enough for you? Do you want to be a Mormon, and marry Rockefeller and Gladstone Dowie and the King of Spain and the whole bunch? Ain't $20,000 a year good enough for you?"

Nancy flushed a little under the level gaze of the black, shallow eyes.

"It wasn't altogether the money, Carrie," she explained. "His friend caught him in a rank lie the other night at dinner. It was about some girl he said he hadn't been to the theater with. Well, I can't stand a liar. Put everything together—I don't like him; and that settles it. When I sell out it's not going to be on any bargain day. I've got to have something that sits up in a chair like a man, anyhow. Yes. I'm looking out for a catch; but it's got to be able to do something more than make a noise like a toy bank."

"The physiopathic ward for yours!" said the brown pompadour, walking away.

These high ideas, if not ideals—Nancy continued to cultivate on $8 per week. She bivouacked on the trail of the great unknown "catch" eating her dry bread and tightening her belt day by day. On her face was the faint, soldierly, sweet, grim smile of the preordained man-hunter. The store was her forest; and many times she raised her rifle at game that seemed broad-antlered and big; but always some deep unerring instinct—perhaps of the huntress, perhaps of the woman—made her hold her fire and take up the trail again.

Lou flourished in the laundry. Out of her $18.50 per week she paid $6 for her room and board. The rest went mainly for clothes. Her opportunities for bettering her taste and manners were few compared with Nancy's. In the steaming laundry there was nothing but work, work and her thoughts of the evening pleasures to come. Many costly and showy fabrics passed under her iron; and it may be that her growing fondness for dress was thus transmitted to her through the conducting metal.

When the day's work was over Dan awaited her outside, her faithful shadow in whatever light she stood.

Sometimes he cast an honest and troubled glance at Lou's clothes that increased in conspicuity rather than in style; but this was no disloyalty; he deprecated the attention they called to her in the streets.

And Lou was no less faithful to her chum. There was a
law that Nancy should go with them on whatever outings
they might take. Dan bore the extra burden heartily and in
good cheer. It might be said that Lou furnished the color,
Nancy the tone, and Dan the weight of the distraction-seek-
ing trio. The escort, in his neat but obviously ready-made
suit, his ready-made tie and unfailing, genial, ready-made
wit never startled or clashed. He was of that good kind that
you are likely to forget while they are present, but remember
distinctly after they are gone.

To Nancy's superior taste the flavor of these ready-made
pleasures was sometimes a little bitter: but she was young,
and youth is a gourmand, when it cannot be a gourmet.

"Dan is always wanting me to marry him right away,"
Lou told her once. "But why should I? I'm independent. I
can do as I please with the money I earn; and he never
would agree for me to keep on working afterward. And say,
Nance, what do you want to stick to that old store for, and
half starve and half dress yourself? I could get you a place in
the laundry right now if you'd come. It seems to me that you
could afford to be a little less stuck-up if you could make a
good deal more money."

"I don't think I'm stuck-up, Lou," said Nancy, "but I'd
rather live on half rations and stay where I am. I suppose
I've got the habit. It's the chance that I want. I don't expect
to be always behind a counter. I'm learning something new
every day. I'm right up against refined and rich people all
the time—even if I do only wait on them; and I'm not missing any pointers that I see passing around."

"Caught your millionaire yet?" asked Lou with her teas-
ing laugh.

"I haven't selected one yet," answered Nancy. "I've been
looking them over."

"Goodness! the idea of picking over 'em! Don't you ever let one get by you, Nance—even if he's a few dollars shy. But of course you're joking—millionaires don't think about working girls like us."

"It might be better for them if they did," said Nancy, with cool wisdom. "Some of us could teach them how to take care of their money."

"If one was to speak to me," laughed Lou, "I know I'd have a duck-fit."

"That's because you don't know any. The only difference between swells and other people is you have to watch 'em closer. Don't you think that red silk lining is just a little bit too bright for that coat, Lou?"

Lou looked at the plain, dull olive jacket of her friend.

"Well, no, I don't—but it may seem so beside that faded-looking thing you've got on."

"This jacket," said Nancy, complacently, "has exactly the cut and fit of one that Mrs. Van Alstyne Fisher was wearing the other day. The material cost me $3.98. I suppose hers cost about $100 more."

"Oh, well," said Lou, lightly, "it don't strike me as millionaire bait. Shouldn't wonder if I catch one before you do, anyway."

Truly it would have taken a philosopher to decide upon the values of the theories held by the two friends. Lou, lacking that certain pride and fastidiousness that keeps stores and desks filled with girls working for the barest living, thumped away gaily with her iron in the noisy and stifling laundry. Her wages supported her even beyond the point of comfort; so that her dress profited until sometimes she cast a sidelong glance of impatience at the neat but inelegant apparel of Dan—Dan the constant, the immutable, the undeviating.

As for Nancy, her case was one of tens of thousands. Silk and jewels and laces and ornaments and the perfume and music of the fine world of good-breeding and taste—these were made for woman; they are her equitable portion. Let her keep near them if they are a part of life to her, and if she will. She is no traitor to herself, as Esau was; for she keeps her birthright and the pottage she earns is often very scant.

In this atmosphere Nancy belonged; and she throve in it and ate her frugal meals and schemed over her cheap dresses with a determined and contented mind. She already knew woman; and she was studying man, the animal, both as to his habits and eligibility. Some day she would bring down the game that she wanted; but she promised herself it would be what seemed to her the biggest and the best, and nothing smaller.

Thus she kept her lamp trimmed and burning to receive the bride-groom when he should come.

But another lesson she learned, perhaps unconsciously. Her standard of values began to shift and change. Sometimes the dollar-mark grew blurred in her mind's eye, and shaped itself into letters that spelled such words as "truth" and "honor" and now and then just "kindness." Let us make a likeness of one who hunts the moose or elk in some mighty wood. He sees a little dell, mossy and embowered, where a rill trickles, babbling to him of rest and comfort. At these times the spear of Nimrod himself grows blunt.

So Nancy wondered sometimes if Persian lamb was always quoted at its market value by the hearts that covered.

One Thursday evening Nancy left the store and turned across Sixth Avenue westward to the laundry. She was expected to go with Lou and Dan to a musical comedy.

Dan was just coming out of the laundry when she arrived.

There was a queer, strained look on his face.

"I thought I would drop around to see if they heard from her," he said.

"Heard from who?" asked Nancy. "Isn't Lou there?"

"I thought you knew," said Dan. "She hasn't been here or at the house where she lived since Monday. She moved all her things from there. She told one of the girls in the laundry she might be going to Europe."

"Hasn't anybody seen her anywhere?" asked Nancy.

Dan looked at her with his jaws set grimly, and a steely gleam in his steady gray eyes.

"They told me in the laundry," he said, harshly, "that they saw her pass yesterday—in an automobile. With one of the millionaires, I suppose, that you and Lou were forever busying your brains about."

For the first time Nancy quailed before a man. She laid her hand that trembled slightly on Dan's sleeve.

"You've no right to say such a thing to me, Dan—as if I had anything to do with it!"

"I didn't mean it that way," said Dan, softening. He fumbled in his vest pocket.

I've got the tickets for the show to-night," he said, with a gallant show of lightness. "If you—"

Nancy admired pluck whenever she saw it.

"Ill go with you, Dan," she said.

Three months went by before Nancy saw Lou again.

At twilight one evening the shop-girl was hurrying home along the border of a little quiet park. She heard her name called, and wheeled about in time to catch Lou rushing into her arms.

After the first embrace they drew their heads back as serpents do, ready to attack or to charm, with a thousand ques-

tions trembling on their swift tongues. And then Nancy
noticed that prosperity had descended upon Lou, manifest-
ing itself in costly furs, flashing gems, and creations of the
tailor's art.

"You little fool!" cried Lou, loudly and affectionately. "I
see you are still working in that store, and as shabby as ever.
And how about that big catch you were going to make—
nothing doing yet, I suppose?"

And then Lou looked, and saw that something better than
prosperity had descended upon Nancy—something that
shone brighter than gems in her eyes and redder than a rose
in her cheeks, and that danced like electricity anxious to be
loosed from the tip of her tongue.

"Yes, I'm still in the store," said Nancy, "but I'm going
to leave it next week. I've made my catch—the biggest catch
in the world. You won't mind now Lou, will you?—I'm going
to be married to Dan—to Dan!—he's my Dan now—why,
Lou!"

Around the corner of the park strolled one of those new-
crop, smooth-faced young policemen that are making the
force more endurable—at least to the eye. He saw a woman
with an expensive fur coat and diamond-ringed hands
crouching down against the iron fence of the park sobbing
turbulently, while a slender, plainly dressed working girl
leaned close, trying to console her. But the Gibsonian cop,
being of the new order, passed on, pretending not to notice,
for he was wise enough to know that these matters are beyond help so far as the power he represents is concerned,
though he rap the pavement with his nightstick till the sound
goes up to the furthermost stars.

FRANKIE MAE

* * * * * * *

* * *

by Jean Wheeler Smith

The sun had just started coming up when the men gathered at the gate of the White Plantation. They leaned on the fence, waiting. No one was nervous, though. They'd all been waiting a long time. A few more minutes couldn't make much difference. They surveyed the land that they were leaving, the land from which they had brought forth seas of cotton.

Old Man Brown twisted around so that he leaned sideways on the gate. Even though he was in his fifties, he was still a handsome man. Medium-sized, with reddish-brown skin. His beard set him apart from the others; it was the same mixture of black and gray as his hair, but while his hair looked like wool, the strands of his beard were long, and nearly straight. He was proud of it, and even when he wasn't able to take a bath, he kept his beard neatly cut and shaped into a V.

He closed his eyes. The sun was getting too bright; it made his headache worse. Damn, he thought, I sure wouldn't be out here this early on no Monday morning if it wasn't for what we got to do today. Whiskey'll sure kill you if you don't get some sleep long with it. I wasn't never just crazy 'bout doing this, anyway. Wonder what made me decide to go along?

Then he smiled to himself. 'Course. It was on account of Frankie Mae. She always getting me into something.

Frankie was his first child, born twenty-two years ago,

during the war. When she was little, she had gone everywhere
with him. He had a blue bicycle with a rusty wire basket
in the front. He used to put Frankie Mae in the basket and
ride her to town with him and to the cafe, and sometimes
they'd go nowhere special, just riding. She'd sit sideways so
that she could see what was on the road ahead and talk with
him at the same time. She never bothered to hold onto the
basket; she knew her daddy wouldn't let her fall. Frankie
fitted so well into the basket that for a few years the Old
Man thought that it was growing with her.

She was a black child, with huge green eyes that seemed
to glow in the dark. From the age of four on, she had a look
of being full-grown. The look was in her muscular, well-
defined limbs that seemed like they could do a woman's
work and in her way of seeing everything around her. Most
times, she was alive and happy. The only thing wrong with
her was that she got hurt so easy. The slightest rebuke sent
her crying; the least hint of disapproval left her moody and
depressed for hours. But on the other side of it was that she
had a way of springing back from pain. No matter how hurt
she had been, she would be her old self by the next day.
The Old Man worried over her. He wanted most to cushion
her life.

When Frankie reached six, she became too large to ride in
the basket with him. Also he had four more children by then.
So he bought a car for $40. Not long afterward, he became
restless. He'd heard about how you could make a lot of
money over in the delta. So he decided to go over there. He
packed what he could carry in one load—the children, a few
chickens, and a mattress—and slipped off one night.

Two days after they left the hills, they drove up to the
White Plantation in Leflore County, Mississippi. They were

given a two-room house that leaned to one side and five dollars to make some groceries with for the next month.

The Old Man and his wife, Mattie, worked hard that year. Up at four-thirty and out to the field. Frankie Mae stayed behind to nurse the other children and to watch the pot that was cooking for dinner. At sundown they came back home and got ready for the next day. They did a little sweeping, snapped some beans for dinner the next day, and washed for the baby. Then they sat on the porch together for maybe a half hour.

That was the time the Old Man liked best, the half hour before bed. He and Frankie talked about what had happened during the day, and he assured her that she had done a good job keeping up the house. Then he went on about how smart she was going to be when she started school. It would be in two years, when the oldest boy was big enough to take care of the others.

One evening on the porch Frankie said, "A man from town come by today looking for our stove. You know, the short one, the one ain't got no hair. Said we was three week behind and he was gonna take it. Had a truck to take it back in, too."

The Old Man lowered his head. He was ashamed that Frankie had had to face that man by herself. No telling what he said to her. And she took everything so serious. He'd have to start teaching her how to deal with folks like that.

"What did you tell him, baby?" he asked. "He didn't hurt you none, did he?"

"No, he didn't bother me, sides looking mean. I told him I just this morning seen some money come in the mail from Uncle Ed in Chicago. And I heard my daddy say he was gonna use it to pay off the stove man. So he said, 'Well, I give y'all one more week, one more.' And he left."

The Old Man pulled Frankie to him and hugged her. "You did 'zactly right, honey." She understood. She would be able to take care of herself.

The end of their first year in the delta, the Old Man and Mattie went to settle up. It was just before Christmas. When their turn came, they were called by Mr. White Junior, a short fat man, with a big stomach, whose clothes were always too tight.

"Let me see, Johnnie," he said. "Here it is. You owe two hundred dollars."

The Old Man was surprised. Sounded just like he was back in the hills. He had expected things to be different over here. He had made a good crop. Should have cleared something. Well, no sense in arguing. The bossman counted out fifty dollars.

"Here's you some Christmas money," Mr. White Junior said. "Pay me when you settle up next year.

The Old Man took the money to town the same day and bought himself some barrels and some pipes and a bag of chopped corn. He had made whiskey in the hills, and he could make it over here, too. You could always find somebody to buy it. Wasn't no reason he should spend all his time farming if he couldn't make nothing out of it. He and Mattie put up their barrels in the trees down by the river and set their mash to fermentate.

By spring, Brown had a good business going. He sold to the colored cafes and even to some of the white ones. And folks knew they could always come to his house if they ran out. He didn't keep the whiskey at the house, though. Too dangerous. It was buried down by the water. When folks came unexpected, it was up to Frankie and her brother next to her to go get the bottles. Nobody noticed children. The Old Man bought them a new red wagon for their job.

He was able to pay off his stove and to give Mattie some money every once in a while. And they ate a little better now. But still they didn't have much more than before, because Brown wasn't the kind of man to save. Also, he had to do a lot of drinking himself to keep up his sales. Folks didn't like to drink by themselves. When he'd start to drinking, he usually spent up or gave away whatever he had in his pocket. So they still had to work as hard as ever for Mr. White Junior. Brown enjoyed selling the whiskey, though, and Mattie could always go out and sell a few bottles in case of some emergency like their lights being cut off. So they kept the business going.

That spring, Mr. White Junior decided to take them off shares: He would pay $1.50 a day for chopping cotton, and he'd pay by the hundred pound for picking. The hands had no choice. They could work by the day or leave. Actually, the Old Man liked it better working by the day. Then he would have more time to see to his whiskey.

Also, Mr. White Junior made Brown the timekeeper over the other hands. Everybody had drunk liquor with him, and most folks liked him. He did fight too much. But the hands knew that he always carried his pistol. If anybody fought him, they'd have to be trying to kill him, 'cause he'd be trying to kill them.

Brown was given a large, battered watch. So he'd know what time to stop for dinner. His job was to see that hands made a full day in the field and that all the weeds got chopped. The job was easier than getting out there chopping, in all that sun. So Brown liked it. The only hard part was in keeping after the women whose time was about to come. He hated to see them dragging to the field, their bellies about to burst. They were supposed to keep up with the others,

which was impossible. Oftentimes, Mr. White Junior slipped
up on the work crew and found one of the big-bellied women
lagging behind the others.

"Goddammit, Johnnie," he'd say. "I done told you to keep
the hands together. Queenester is way behind. I don't pay
good money for folks to be standing around. If she sick, she
need to go home."

Sometimes the Old Man felt like defending the woman.
She had done the best she could. But then he'd think, No,
better leave things like they is.

"You sure right, Mr. White Junior. I was just 'bout to
send her home myself. Some niggers too lazy to live."

He would walk slowly across the field to the woman. "I'm
sorry, Queenester. The bossman done seen you. I told you
all to be looking out for him! Now you got to go. You come
back tomorrow, though. He won't hardly be back in this
field so soon. I try and let you make two more days this
week. I know you need the little change."

The woman would take up her hoe and start walking
home. Mr. White Junior didn't carry no hands except to
eat dinner and to go home after the day had been made.

One day when he had carried the hands in from the field,
Mr. White Junior stopped the Old Man as he was climbing
down from the back of the pickup truck. While the bossman talked, Brown fingered his timekeeper's watch that
hung on a chain from his belt.

"Johnnie," Mr. White Junior said, "it don't look right to
me for you to leave a girl at home that could be working
when I need all the hands I can get. And you the timekeeper,
too. This cotton can't wait on you all to get ready to chop
it. I want Frankie Mae out there tomorrow."

He had tried to resist. "But we getting along with what

* * * *

me and Mattie makes. Ain't got nothing, but we eating. I wants Frankie Mae to go to school. We can do without the few dollars she would make."

"I want my cotton chopped." White said, swinging his fat, sweating body into the truck. "Get that girl down here tomorrow. Don't nobody stay in my house and don't work."

That night the Old Man dreaded the half hour on the porch. When Frankie had started school that year, she had already been two years late. And she had been so excited about going.

When the wood had been gathered and the children cleaned up, he followed Frankie onto the sloping porch. She fell to telling him about the magnificent yellow bus in which she rode to school. He sat down next to her on the step.

"Frankie Mae, I'm going to tell you something."

"What's that, Daddy? Mama say I been slow 'bout helping 'round the house since I been going to school? I do better. Guess I lost my head."

"No, baby. That aint it at all. You been helping your mama fine." He stood up to face her but could not bring his eyes to the level of her bright, happy face.

"Mr. White Junior stopped me today when I was getting off the truck. Say he want you to come to field till the chopping get done."

She found his eyes. "What did you say, Daddy?"

"Well, I told him you wanted to go to school, and we could do without your little money. But he say you got to go."

The child's eyes lost their brilliance. Her shoulders slumped, and she began to cry softly. Tired, the Old Man sat back down on the step. He took her hand and sat with her until long after Mattie and the other children had gone to bed.

The next morning, Frankie was up first. She put on two blouses and a dress and some pants to keep off the sun and found herself a rag to tie around her head. Then she woke up her daddy and the others, scolding them for being so slow.

"We got to go get all that cotton chopped! And ya'll laying round wasting good daylight. Come on."

Brown got up and threw some water on his face. Here was Frankie bustling around in her layers of clothes, looking like a little old woman, and he smiled. That's how Frankie Mae was. She'd feel real bad, terrible, for a few hours, but she always snapped back. She'd be all right now.

On the way to the field he said, "Baby, I'm gonna make you the water girl. All you got to do is carry water over to them that hollers for it and keep your bucket full. You don't have to chop none lest you see Mr. White Junior coming."

"No, Daddy, that's all right. The other hands'll say you was letting me off easy 'cause I'm yours. Say you taking advantage of being timekeeper. I go on and chop with the rest."

He tried to argue with her, but she wouldn't let him give her the water bucket. Finally, he put her next to Mattie so she could learn from her. As he watched over the field, he set himself not to think about his child inhaling the cotton dust and insecticide. When his eyes happened on her and Mattie, their backs bent way over, he quickly averted them. Once when he jerked his eyes away, he found instead the bright-yellow school bus bouncing along the road.

Frankie learned quickly how to chop the cotton, and sometimes she even seemed to enjoy herself. Often the choppers would go to the store to buy sardines and crackers and beans for their dinner instead of going home. At the store the Old Man would eat his beans from their jagged-edge can

* * * *

and watch with pride as Frankie laughed and talked with everyone and made dates with the ladies to attend church on the different plantations. Every Sunday, Frankie had a service to go to. Sometimes, when his head wasn't bad from drinking, the Old Man went with her, because he liked so much to see her enjoy herself. Those times, he put a few gallons of his whiskey in the back of the car just in case somebody needed them. When he and Frankie went off to church like that, they didn't usually get back till late that night. They would be done sold all the whiskey and the Old Man would be talking loud about the wonderful sermon that the reverend had preached and all the souls that had come to Jesus.

That year, they finished the chopping in June. It was too late to send Frankie back to school, and she couldn't go again until after the cotton had been picked. When she went back, in November, she had missed four months and found it hard to keep up with the children who'd been going all the time. Still, she went every day that she could. She stayed home only when she had to, when her mother was sick, or when, in the cold weather, she didn't have shoes to wear.

Whenever she learned that she couldn't go to school on a particular day, she withdrew into herself for about an hour. She had a chair near the stove where she sat, and the little children knew not to bother her. After the hour, she'd push back her chair and go to stirring the cotton in the bed ticks or washing the greens for dinner.

If this was possible, the Old Man loved her still more now. He saw the children of the other workers and his own children, too, get discouraged and stop going to school. They said it was too confusing, they never knew what the teacher was talking about, because they'd not been there the day before or the month before. And they resented being left behind in classes with children half their size. He saw the other children get so that they wouldn't hold themselves up, wouldn't try to be clean and make folks respect them. Yet, every other day, Frankie managed to put on a clean, starched dress, and she kept at her lessons.

By the time Frankie was thirteen, she could figure as well as the preacher, and she was made secretary of the church.

That same year, she asked her daddy if she could keep a record of what they made and what they spent.

"Sure, baby," he said. "I be proud for you to do it. We might even come out a little better this year when we settle up. I tell you what. If we get money outta Mr. White Junior this year, I'll buy you a dress for Christmas, a red one."

Frankie bought a black-and-white-speckled notebook. She put in it what they made and what they paid out on their bills. After chopping time, she became excited. She figured that they had just about paid the bill out. What they made from picking would be theirs. She and the Old Man would sit on the porch and go over the figures and plan for Christmas. Sometimes they even talked about taking a drive up to Chicago to see Uncle Ed. Every so often, he would try to hold down her excitement by reminding her that their figures had to be checked by the bossman's. Actually, he didn't expect to do much better than he'd done all the other years. But she was so proud to be using what she had learned, her numbers and all. He hated to discourage her.

Just before Christmas, they went to settle up. When it came to the Old Man's turn, he trembled a little. He knew it was almost too much to hope for, that they would have money coming to them. But some of Frankie's excitement had rubbed off on him.

He motioned to her, and they went up to the table, where there were several stacks of ten and twenty dollar bills, a big ledger, and a pistol. Mr. White Junior sat in the brown chair, and his agent stood behind him. Brown took heart from the absolute confidence with which Frankie Mae walked next to him, and he controlled his trembling. Maybe the child was right and they had something coming to them.

"Hey there, Johnnie," Mr. White Junior said, "see you brought Frankie Mae along. Fine, fine. Good to start them early. Here's you a seat."

The Old Man gave Frankie the one chair and stood beside her. The bossman rifled his papers and came out with a long, narrow sheet. Brown recognized his name at the top.

"Here you are, Johnnie, y'all come out pretty good this year. Proud of you. Don't owe but $65. Since you done so good, gonna let you have $100 for Christmas."

Frankie Mae spoke up. "I been keeping a book for my daddy. And I got some different figures. Let me show you."

The room was still. Everyone, while pretending not to notice the girl, was listening intently to what she said.

Mr. White Junior looked surprised, but he recovered quickly. "Why sure. Be glad to look at your figures. You know it's easy to make a mistake. I'll show you what you done wrong."

Brown clutched her shoulder to stop her from handing over the book. But it was too late. Already she was leaning over the table, comparing her figures with those in the ledger.

"See, Mr. White Junior, when we was chopping last year we made $576, and you took $320 of that to put on our bill. There. There it is on your book. And we borrowed $35 in July. There it is . . ."

The man behind the table grew red. One of his fat hands gripped the table while the other moved toward the pistol.

Frankie Mae finished. "So you see, you owe us $180 for the year."

The bossman stood up to gain the advantage of his height. He seemed about to burst. His eyes flashed around the room, and his hand clutched the pistol. He was just raising it from the table when he caught hold of himself. He took a deep breath and let go of the gun.

"Oh, yeah. I remember what happened now, Johnnie. It was the slip I gave you to the doctor for Willie B. You remember, last year, 'fore chopping time. I got the bill last week. Ain't had time to put it in my book. It came to, let me think. Yeah, that was the $350."

The Old Man's tension fell away from him, and he resumed his normal manner. He knew exactly what the bossman was saying. It was as he had expected, as it had always been.

"Let's go, baby," he said.

But Frankie didn't get up from the chair. For a moment, she looked puzzled. Then her face cleared. She said, "Willie didn't have anything wrong with him but a broken arm. The doctor spent twenty minutes with him one time and ten the other. That couldn't a cost no $350!"

The bossman's hand found the pistol again and gripped it until the knuckles were white. Brown pulled Frankie to

him and put his arm around her. With his free hand he
fingered his own pistol, which he always carried in his
pocket. He was not afraid. But he hated the thought of
shooting the man; even if he just nicked him, it would be the
end for himself. He drew a line. If Mr. White Junior
touched him or Frankie, he would shoot. Short of that, he
would leave without a fight.

White spat thick, brown tobacco juice onto the floor,
spattering it on the Old Man and the girl. "Nigger," he
said, "I know you ain't disputing my word. Don't nobody
live on my place and call me a liar. That bill was $350.
You understand me?!" He stood tense, staring with hatred
at the man and the girl. Everyone waited for Brown to
answer. The Old Man felt Frankie's arms go 'round his
waist.

"Tell him no, Daddy. We right, not him. I kept them
figures all year, they got to be right." The gates of the state
farm flashed through the Old Man's mind. He thought of
Mattie, already sick from high blood, trying to make a living
for eleven people. Frankie's arms tightened.

"Yessir," he said. "I understand."

The girl's arms dropped from him, and she started to
the door. The other workers turned away to fiddle with a
piece of rope to scold a child. Brown accepted the $50 that
was thrown across the table to him. As he turned to follow
Frankie, he heard Mr. White Junior's voice, low now and
with a controlled violence. "Hey you, girl. You, Frankie
Mae." She stopped at the door but didn't turn around.

"Long as you live, bitch, I'm gonna be right and you
gonna be wrong. Now get your black ass outta here."

Frankie stumbled out to the car and crawled onto the
back seat. She cried all the way home. Brown tried to

quiet her. She could still have the red dress. They'd go
down to the river tomorrow and start on a new batch of
whiskey.

The next morning, he lay in bed waiting to hear Frankie
Mae moving around and fussing, waiting to know that she
had snapped back to her old self. He lay there until everyone in the house had gotten up. Still he did not hear her.
Finally, he got up and went over to where she was balled
up in the quilts.

He woke her. "Come on, baby. Time to get up. School
bus be here soon."

"I ain't goin' today," she said; "got a stomach-ache."

Brown sat on the porch all day long, wishing that she
would get up out the bed and struggling to understand what
had happened. This time, Frankie had not bounced back to
her old bright self. The line that held her to this self had
been stretched too taut. It had lost its tension and couldn't
pull her back.

Frankie never again kept a book for her daddy. She lost
interest in things such as numbers and reading. She went to
school as an escape from chores but got so little of her lessons done that she was never promoted from the fourth grade
to the fifth. When she was fifteen, and in the fourth grade,
she had her first child. After that, there was no more thought
of school. In the following four years she had three more
children.

She sat around the house, eating and growing fat. When
well enough, she went to the field with her daddy. Her dresses
were seldom ironed now. Whatever she could find to wear
would do.

Still, there were a few times, maybe once every three or
four months, when she was lively and fresh. She'd get

* * * *

dressed and clean the children up and have her daddy drive them to church. On such days she'd be the first one up. She would have food on the stove before anybody else had a chance to dress. Brown would load up his truck with his whiskey, and they'd stay all day.

It was for these isolated times that the Old Man waited. They kept him believing that she would get to be all right. Until she died, he woke up every morning listening for her laughter, waiting for her to pull the covers from his feet and scold him for being lazy.

She died giving birth to her fifth child. The midwife, Esther, was good enough, but she didn't know what to do when there were complications. Brown couldn't get up but sixty dollars of the hundred dollars cash that you had to deposit at the county hospital. So they wouldn't let Frankie in. She bled to death on the hundred mile drive to the charity hospital in Vicksburg.

The Old Man squinted up at the fully risen sun. The bossman was late. Should have been at the gate by now. Well, it didn't matter. Just a few more minutes and they'd be through with the place forever.

His thoughts went back to the time when the civil rights workers had first come around and they had started their meetings up at the store. They'd talked about voting and about how plantation workers should be making enough to live off of. Brown and the other men had listened and talked and agreed. So they decided to ask Mr. White Junior for a raise. They wanted nine dollars for their twelve-hour day.

They had asked. And he had said, Hell no. Before he'd raise them he'd lower them. So they agreed to ask him again. And if he still said no, they would go on strike.

At first, Brown hadn't understood himself why he agreed

to the strike. It was only this morning that he realized why: It wasn't the wages or the house that was falling down 'round him and Mattie. It was that time when he went to ask Mr. White Junior about the other forty dollars that he needed to put Frankie in the hospital.

"Sorry, Johnnieboy," he'd said, patting Brown on the back, "but me and Miz White have a garden party today and I'm so busy. You know how women are. She want me there every minute. See me tomorrow. I'll fix you up then."

A cloud of dust rose up in front of Brown. The bossman was barreling down the road in his pickup truck. He was mad. That was what he did when he got mad, drove his truck up and down the road fast. Brown chuckled. When they got through with him this morning, he might run that truck into the river.

Mr. White Junior climbed down from the truck and made his way over to the gate. He began to give the orders for the day, who would drive the tractors, what fields would be chopped. The twelve men moved away from the fence, disdaining any support for what they were about to do.

One of the younger ones, James Lee, spoke up. "Mr. White Junior, we wants to know is you gonna raise us like we asked."

"No, goddammit. Now go on, do what I told you."

"Then," James Lee continued, "we got to go on strike from this place."

James Lee and the others left the gate and went to have a strategy meeting up at the store about what to do next.

The Old Man was a little behind the rest because he had something to give Mr. White Junior. He went over to the sweat-drenched, cursing figure and handed him the scarred timekeeper's watch, the watch that had ticked away Frankie Mae's youth in the hot, endless rows of cotton.

THE TONE OF TIME

* * * * * * * *

* * * * *

by Henry James

ONE

I was too pleased with what it struck me that, as an old, old friend, I had done for her, not to go to her that very afternoon with the news. I knew she worked late, as in general I also did; but I sacrificed for her sake a good hour of the February daylight. She was in her studio, as I had believed she would be, where her card ("Mary J. Tredick"— not Mary Jane, but Mary Juliana) was manfully on the door; a little tired, a little old and a good deal spotted, but with her ugly spectacles taken off, as soon as I appeared, to greet me. She kept on, while she scraped her palette and wiped her brushes, the big stained apron that covered her from head to foot and that I have often enough before seen her retain in conditions giving the measures of her renunciation of her desire to dazzle. Every fresh reminder of this brought home to me that she had given up everything but her work, and that there had been in her history some reason. But I was as far from the reason as ever. She had given up too much; this was just why one wanted to lend her a hand. I told her, at any rate, that I had a lovely job for her.

"To copy something I do like?"

Her complaint, I knew, was that people only gave orders, if they gave them at all, for things she did not like. But this wasn't a case of copying—not at all, at least, in the common sense. "It's for a portrait—quite in the air."

"Ah, you do portraits yourself!"

"Yes, and you know how. My trick won't serve for this. What's wanted is a pretty picture."

"Then of whom?"

"Of nobody. That is of anybody. Anybody you like."

She naturally wondered. "Do you mean I'm myself to choose my sitter?"

"Well, the oddity is that there is to *be* no sitter."

"Whom then is the picture to represent?"

"Why, a handsome, distinguished, agreeable man, of not more than forty, clean-shaven, thoroughly well-dressed, and a perfect gentleman."

She continued to stare. "And I'm to find him myself?"

I laughed at the term she used. "Yes, as you 'find' the canvas, the colours and the frame." After which I immediately explained. "I've just had the 'rummest' visit, the effect of which was to make me think of you. A lady, unknown to me and unintroduced, turned up at my place at three o'clock. She had come straight, she let me know, without preliminaries, on account of one's high reputation—the usual thing —and of her having admired one's work. Of course I instantly saw—I mean I saw it as soon as she named her affair—that she hadn't understood my work at all. What am I good for in the world but just the impression of the given, the presented case? I can do but the face I see."

"And do you think I can do the face I don't?"

"No, but you see so many more. You see them in fancy and memory, and they've come out, for you, from all the museums you've haunted and all the great things you've studied. I *know* you'll be able to see the one my visitor wants and to give it—what's the *crux* of the business—the tone of time."

She turned the question over. "What does she want it for?"

"Just *for* that—for the tone of time. And, except that it's
to hang over her chimney, she didn't tell me. I've only my
idea that it's to represent, to symbolise, as it were, her husband, who's not alive and who perhaps never was. This is
exactly what will give you a free hand."

"With nothing to go by—no photographs or other portraits?"

"Nothing."

"She only proposes to describe him?"

"Not even; she wants the picture itself to do that. Her
only condition is that he be a *très-bel homme*."

She had begun at last, a little thoughtfully, to remove her
apron. "Is she French?"

"I don't know. I give it up. She calls herself Mrs. Bridgenorth."

Mary wondered. *"Connais pas!* I never heard of her."

"You wouldn't."

"You mean it's not her real name?"

I hesitated. "I mean that she's a very downright fact, full
of the implication that she'll pay a downright price. It's
clear to me that you can ask what you like; and it's therefore a chance that I can't consent to your missing." My
friend gave no sign either way, and I told my story. "She's
a woman of fifty, perhaps of more, who has been pretty, and
who still presents herself, with her grey hair a good deal
powdered, as I judge, to carry it off, extraordinarily well. She
was a little frightened and a little free; the latter because of
the former. But she did uncommonly well, I thought, considering the oddity of her wish. This oddity she quite admits;
she began indeed by insisting on it so in advance that I found
myself expecting I didn't know what. She broke at moments
into French, which was perfect, but no better than her

English, which isn't vulgar; not more at least than that of everybody else. The things people *do* say, and the way they say them, to artists! She wanted immensely, I could see, not to fail of her errand, not to be treated as absurd; and she was extremely grateful to me for meeting her so far as I did. She was beautifully dressed and she came in a braugham."

My listener took it in; then, very quietly, "Is she respectable?" she inquired.

"Ah, there you are!" I laughed; "and how you always pick the point right out, even when one has endeavoured to diffuse a specious glamour! She's extraordinary," I pursued after an instant; "and just what she wants of the picture, I think, is to make her a little less so."

"Who is she, then? What is she?" my companion simply went on.

It threw me straight back on one of my hobbies. "Ah, my dear, what is so interesting as life? What is, above all, so stupendous as London? There's everything in it, everything in the world, and nothing too amazing not some day to pop out at you. What is a woman, faded, preserved, pretty, powdered, vague, odd, dropping on one without credentials, but with a carriage and very good lace? What is such a person but a person who *may* have had adventures, and have made them, in one way or another pay? They're, however, none of one's business; it's scarcely on the cards that one should ask her. I should like, with Mrs. Bridgenorth, to see a fellow ask! She goes in for propriety, the real thing. If I suspect her of being the creation of her own talents, she has clearly, on the other hand, seen a lot of life. Will you meet her?" I next demanded.

My hostess waited. "No."

"Then you won't try?"

"Need I meet her to try?" And the question made me guess that, so far as she had understood, she began to feel herself a little taken. "It seems strange," she none the less mused, "to attempt to please her on such a basis. To attempt," she presently added, "to please her at all. It's your idea that she's not married?" she, with this, a trifle inconsequently asked.

"Well," I replied, "I've only had an hour to think of it, but I somehow already see the scene. Not immediately, not the day after, or even perhaps the year after the thing she desires is set up there, but in due process of time and on convenient opportunity, the transfiguration will occur. 'Who is that awfully handsome man?' 'That? Oh, that's an old sketch of my dear dead husband.' Because I told her—insidiously sounding her—that she would want it to look old, and that the tone of time is exactly what you're full of."

"I believe I am," Mary sighed at last.

"Then put on your hat." I had proposed to her on my arrival to come out to tea with me, and it was when left alone in the studio while she went to her room that I began to feel sure of the success of my errand. The vision that had an hour before determined me grew deeper and brighter for her while I moved about and looked at her things. There were more of them there on her hands than one liked to see; but at least they sharpened my confidence, which was pleasant for me in view of that of my visitor, who had accepted without reserve my plea for Miss Tredick. Four or five of her copies of famous portraits—ornaments of great public and private collections—were on the walls, and to see them again together was to feel at ease about my guarantee. The mellow manner of them was what I had had in my mind in saying, to excuse myself to Mrs. Bridgenorth, "Oh, my things, you know, look as if they had been painted tomorrow!" It made no difference that Mary's Vandykes and Gainsboroughs were reproductions and replicas, for I had known her more than once to amuse herself with doing the thing quite, as she called it, off her own bat. She had copied so bravely so many brave things that she had at the end of her brush an extraordinary bag of tricks. She had always replied to me that such things were mere clever humbug, but mere clever humbug was what our client happened to want. The thing was to let her have it—one could trust her for the rest. And at the same time that I mused in this way I observed to myself that there was already something more than, as the phrase is, met the eye in such response as I felt my friend had made. I had touched, without intention, more than one spring; I had set in motion more than one impulse. I found myself indeed quite certain of this after she had come back in her hat and her jacket. She was different—her idea had flowered; and she smiled at me from under her tense veil, while she drew over her firm, narrow hands a pair of fresh gloves, with a light distinctly new. "Please tell your friend that I'm greatly obliged to both of you and that I take the order."

"Good. And to give him all his good looks?"

"It's just to do *that* that I accept. I shall make him supremely beautiful—and supremely base."

"Base?" I just demurred.

"The finest gentleman you'll ever have seen, and the worst friend."

I wondered, as I was startled; but after an instant I laughed for joy. "Ah well, so long as he's not mine! I see we *shall* have him," I said as we went, for truly I had touched a spring. In fact I had touched *the* spring.

It rang, more or less, I was presently to find, all over the place. I went, as I had promised, to report to Mrs. Bridge-

north on my mission, and though she declared herself much
gratified at the success of it I could see she a little resented
the apparent absence of any desire on Miss Tredick's part
for a preliminary conference. "I only thought she might have
liked just to see me, and have imagined I might like to see
her."

But I was full of comfort. "You'll see her when it's
finished. You'll see her in time to thank her."

"And to pay her, I suppose," my hostess laughed, with an
asperity that was, after all, not excessive. "Will she take
very long?"

I thought. "She's so full of it that my impression would be
that she'll do it off at a heat."

"She *is* full of it then?" she asked; and on hearing to what
tune, though I told her but half, she broke out with admiration. "You artists are the most extraordinary people!" It
was almost with a bad conscience that I confessed we indeed
were, and while she said that what she meant was that we
seemed to understand everything, and I rejoined that this
was also what *I* meant, she took me into another room to
see the place for the picture—a proceeding of which the
effect was singularly to confirm the truth in question. The
place for the picture—in her own room, as she called it, a
boudoir at the back, overlooking the general garden of the
approved modern row and, as she said, only just wanting
that touch—proved exactly the place (the space of a large
panel in the white woodwork over the mantel) that I had
spoken of to my friend. She put it quite candidly, "Don't
you see what it will do?" and looked at me, wonderfully,
as for a sign that I could sympathetically take from her what
she didn't literally say. She said it, poor woman, so very
nearly that I had no difficulty whatever. The portrait,
tastefully enshrined there, of the finest gentleman one should

ever have seen, would do even more for herself than it would do for the room.

I may as well mention at once that my observation of Mrs. Bridgenorth was not in the least of a nature to unseat me from the hobby I have already named. In the light of the impression she made on me life seemed quite as prodigious and London quite as amazing as I had ever contended, and nothing could have been more in the key of that experience than the manner in which everything was vivid between us and nothing expressed. We remained on the surface with the tenacity of shipwrecked persons clinging to a plank. Our plank was our concentrated gaze at Mrs. Bridgenorth's mere present. We allowed her past to exist for us only in the form of the prettiness that she had gallantly rescued from it and to which a few scraps of its identity still adhered. She was amiable, gentle, consistently proper. She gave me more than anything else the sense, simply of waiting. She was like a house so freshly and successfully "done up" that you were surprised it wasn't occupied. She was waiting for something to happen—for somebody to come. She was waiting above all, for Mary Tredick's work. She clearly counted that it would help her.

I had foreseen the fact—the picture was produced at a heat; rapidly, directly, at all events, for the sort of thing it proved to be. I left my friend alone at first, left the ferment to work, troubling her with no questions and asking her for no news; two or three weeks passed, and I never went near her. Then at last, one afternoon as the light was failing, I looked in. She immediately knew what I wanted. "Oh yes, I'm doing him."

"Well," I said, "I've respected your intensity, but I *have* felt curious."

I may not perhaps say that she was never so sad as when

she laughed, but it's certain that she always laughed when she was sad. When, however, poor dear, for that matter, was she secretly, not? Her little gasps of mirth were the mark of her worst moments. But why should she have one of these just now? "Oh, I know your curiosity!" she replied to me; and the small chill of her amusement scarcely met it. "He's coming out, but I can't show him to you yet. I must muddle it through in my own way. It has insisted on being, after all, a 'likeness,'" she added. "But nobody will ever know."

"Nobody?"

"Nobody *she* sees."

"Ah, she doesn't, poor thing." I returned, "seem to see anybody!"

"So much the better. I'll risk it." On which I felt I should have to wait, though I had suddenly grown impatient. But I still hung about, and while I did so she explained. "If what I've done is really a portrait, the condition itself prescribed it. If I was to do the most beautiful man in the world I could do but one."

We looked at each other; then I laughed. "It can scarcely be *me!* But you're getting," I asked, "the great thing?"

"The infamy? Oh yes, please God."

It took away my breath a little, and I even for the moment, scarce felt at liberty to press. But one could always be cheerful. "What I meant is the tone of time."

"Getting it, my dear man? Didn't I get it long ago? Don't I *show* it—the tone of time?" she suddenly, strangely sighed at me, with something in her face I had never yet seen. "I can't give it to him more than—for all these years—he was to have given it to *me*."

I scarce knew what smothered passion, what remembered wrong, what mixture of joy and pain my words had accidentally quickened. Such an effect of them could only become, for me, an instant pity, which, however, I brought out but indirectly. "It's the tone," I smiled, "in which you're speaking now."

This served, unfortunately, as something of a check. "I didn't mean to speak now." Then with her eyes on the picture, "I've said everything there. Come back," she added, "in three days. He'll be all right."

He was indeed when at last I saw him. She had produced an extraordinary thing—a thing wonderful, ideal, for the part it was to play. My only reserve, from the first, was that it was too fine for its part, that something much less "sincere" would equally have served Mrs. Bridgenorth's purpose, and that relegation to that lady's "own room"— whatever charm it was to work there—might only mean for it cruel obscurity. The picture is before me now, so that I could describe it if description availed. It represents a man of about five-and-thirty, seen only as to the head and shoulders, but dressed, the observer gathers, in a fashion now almost antique and which was far from contemporaneous with the date of the work. His high, slightly narrow face, which would be perhaps too aquiline but for the beauty of the forehead and the sweetness of the mouth, has a charm that even, after all these years, still stirs my imagination. His type has altogether a distinction that you feel to have been firmly caught and yet not vulgarly emphasised. The eyes are just too near together, but they are, in a wondrous way, both careless and intense, while lip, cheek, and chin, smooth and clear, are admirably drawn. Youth is still, you see, in all his presence, the joy and pride of life, the perfection of a high spirit and the expectation of a good fortune, which he takes for granted with unconscious insolence. Nothing has ever happened to humiliate or disappoint him, and if my fancy doesn't run away with me the whole presentation of him is a guarantee that he will die without having suffered. He is so handsome in short, that you can scarcely say what he means, and so happy that you can scarcely guess what he feels.

It is of course, I hasten to add, an appreciably feminine rendering, light, delicate, vague, imperfectly synthetic—insistent and evasive, above all, in the wrong places; but the composition, none the less, is beautiful and the suggestion infinite. The grandest air of the thing struck me in fact, when first I saw it, as coming from the high artistic impertinence with which it offered itself as painted about 1850. It would have been a rare flower of refinement for that dark day. The "tone"—that of such a past as it pretended to— was there almost to excess, a brown bloom into which the image seemed mysteriously to retreat. The subject of it looks at me now across more years and more knowledge, but what I felt at the moment was that he managed to be at once a triumphant trick and a plausible evocation. He hushed me, I remember, with so many kinds of awe that I shouldn't have dreamt of asking who he was. All I said, after my first incoherences of wonder at my friend's practised skill, was: "And you've arrived at this truth without documents?"

"It depends what you call documents."

"Without notes, sketches, studies?"

"I destroyed them years ago."

"Then you once had them?"

She just hung fire. "I once had everything."

It told me both more and less than I had asked; enough at all events to make my next question, as I uttered it, sound even to myself a little foolish. "So that it's all memory?"

From where she stood she looked once more at her work; after which she jerked away and, taking several steps, came back to me with something new—whatever it was I had already seen—in her air and answer. "It's all *hate!*" she threw at me, and then went out of the room. It was not till she had gone that I quite understood why. Extremely affected by the impression visibly made on me, she had burst into tears but had wished me not to see them. She left me alone for some time with her wonderful subject, and I again, in her absence, made things out. He was dead—he had been dead for years; the sole humiliation, as I have called it, that he was to know had come to him in that form. The canvas held and cherished him, in any case, as it only holds the dead. She had suffered from him, it came to me, the worst that a woman can suffer, and the wound he had dealt her, though hidden, had never effectually headed. It had bled again while she worked. Yet when she at last reappeared there was but one thing to say. "The beauty, heaven knows, I see. But I don't see what you call the infamy."

She gave him a last look—again she turned away. "Oh, he was like that."

"Well, whatever he was like," I remember replying, "I wonder you can bear to part with him. Isn't it better to let her see the picture first here?"

As to this she doubted. "I don't think I want her to come."

I wondered. "You continue to object so to meet her?"

"What good will it do? It's quite impossible. I should alter him for her."

"Oh, she won't want *that!*" I laughed. "She'll adore him as he is."

"Are you quite sure of your idea?"

"That he's to figure as Mr. Bridgenorth? Well, if I hadn't

* * * *

been from the first, my dear lady, I should be now. Fancy, with the chance, her *not* jumping at him! Yes, he'll figure as Mr. Bridgenorth."

"Mr. Bridgenorth!" she echoed, making the sound, with her small, cold laugh, grotesquely poor for him. He might really have been a prince, and I wondered if he hadn't been. She had, at all events, a new notion. "Do you mind my having it taken to your place and letting her come to see it there?" Which—as I immediately embraced her proposal, deferring to her reasons, whatever they were—was what was speedily arranged.

TWO

The next day therefore I had the picture in charge, and on the following Mrs. Bridgenorth, whom I had notified, arrived. I had placed it, framed and on an easel, well in evidence, and I have never forgotten the look and the cry that, as she became aware of it, leaped into her face and from her lips. It was an extraordinary moment, all the more that it found me quite unprepared—so extraordinary that I scarce knew at first what had happened. By the time I really perceived, moreover, more things had happened than one, so that when I pulled myself together it was to face the situation as a whole. She had recognized on the instant the subject; that came first and was irrepressibly vivid in her. Her recognition had, for the length of a flash, lighted for her the possibility that the stroke had been directed. That came second, and she flushed with it as with a blow in the face. What came third—and it was what was really most wondrous—was the quick instinct of getting both her strange recognition and her blind suspicion well in hand. She couldn't control, however, poor woman, the strong colour in her face and the quick tears in her eyes. She could only glare at the canvas, gasping, grimacing, and try to gain time. Whether in surprise or in resentment she intensely reflected, feeling more than anything else how little she might prudently show; and I was conscious even at the moment that nothing of its kind could have been finer than her effort to swallow her shock in ten seconds.

How many seconds she took I didn't measure; enough, assuredly, for me also to profit. I gained more time than she, and the greatest oddity doubtless was my own private manœuvre—the quicker calculation that, acting from a mere confused instinct, I had ever made. If she had known the great gentleman represented there and yet had determined on the spot to carry herself as ignorant, all my loyalty to Mary Tredick came to the surface in a prompt counter-move. What gave me opportunity was the red in her cheek. "Why, you've known him!"

I saw her ask herself for an instant if she mightn't successfully make her startled state pass as the mere glow of pleasure—her natural greeting to her acquisition. She was pathetically, yet at the same time almost comically, divided. Her line was so to cover her tracks that every avowal of a past connection was a danger; but it also concerned her safety to learn, in the light of our astounding coincidence, how far she already stood exposed. She meanwhile begged the question. She smiled through her tears. "He's too magnificent!"

But I gave her, as I say, all too little time. "Who is he? Who *was* he?"

It must have been my look still more than my words that determined her. She wavered but an instant longer, panted, laughed, cried again, and then, dropping into the nearest seat, gave herself up so completely that I was almost ashamed. "Do you think I'd tell you his *name?*" The burden of the backward years—all the effaced and ignored—lived again, almost like an accent unlearned but freshly breaking out at a touch, in the very sound of the words. These perceptions she, however, the next thing showed me, were a game at which two could play. She had to look at me but an instant. "Why, you really *don't* know it!"

I judged best to be frank. "I don't know it."

"Then how does *she?*"

"How do you?" I laughed. "I'm a different matter."

She sat a minute turning things round, staring at the picture. "The likeness, the likeness!" It was almost too much.

"It's so true?"

"Beyond everything."

I considered. "But a resemblance to a known individual—that wasn't what you wanted."

She sprang up at this in eager protest. "Ah, no one else would see it."

I showed again, I fear, my amusement. "No one but you and she?"

"It's her doing *him!*" She was held by her wonder. "Doesn't she, on your honour, know?"

"That his is the very head you would have liked if you had dared? Not a bit. How *should* she? She knows nothing—on my honour."

Mrs. Bridgenorth continued to marvel. "She just painted him for the kind of face—?"

"That corresponds with my description of what you wished? Precisely."

"But *how*—after so long? From memory? As a friend?"

"As a reminiscence—yes. Visual memory, you see, in our uncanny race, is wonderful. As the ideal thing, simply, for your purpose. You *are* then suited?" I, after an instant added.

She had again been gazing, and at this turned her eyes on me; but I saw she couldn't speak, couldn't do more at least than sound, unutterably, "Suited!" so that I was positively not surprised when suddenly—just as Mary had done, the power to produce this effect seeming a property of the model —she burst into tears. I feel no harsher in relating it, however I may appear, than I did at the moment, but it is a fact that while she just wept I literally had a fresh inspiration on behalf of Miss Tredick's interests. I knew exactly, moreover, before my companion had recovered herself, what she would next ask me; and I consciously brought this appeal on in order to have it over. I explained that I had not the least idea of the identity of our artist's sitter, to which she had given me no clue. I had nothing but my impression that she had known him—known him well; and from whatever material she had worked, the fact of his having also been known to Mrs. Bridgenorth was a coincidence pure and simple. It partook of the nature of prodigy, but such prodigies did occur. My visitor listened with avidity and credulity. She was so far reassured. Then I saw her question come. "Well, if she doesn't dream he was ever anything to me—or what he will be now—I'm going to ask you, as a very particular favour, never to tell her. She will want to know of course exactly how I've been struck. You'll naturally say that I'm delighted, but may I exact from you that you say nothing else?"

There was supplication in her face, but I had to think.

"There are conditions I must put to you first, and one of them is also a question, only more frank than yours. Was this mysterious personage—frustrated by death—to have married you?"

She met it bravely. "Certainly, if he had lived."

I was only amused at an artlessness in her "certainly." "Very good. But why do you wish the coincidence—"

"Kept from her?" She knew exactly why. "Because if she suspects it she won't let me have the picture. Therefore," she added with decision, "you must let me pay for it on the spot."

"What do you mean by on the spot?"

"I'll send you a cheque as soon as I get home."

"Oh," I laughed, "let us understand. Why do you consider she won't let you have the picture?"

She made me wait a little for this, but when it came it was perfectly lucid. "Because she'll then see how much more *I* must want it."

"How much less—wouldn't it be rather, since the bargain was, as the more convenient thing, not for a likeness?"

"Oh," said Mrs. Bridgenorth with impatience, "the likeness will take care of itself. She'll put this and that together." Then she brought out her real apprehension. "She'll be jealous."

"Oh!" I laughed. But I was startled.

"She'll hate me!"

I wondered. "But I don't think she liked him."

"Don't think?" She stared at me, with her echo, over all that might be in it, then seemed to find little enough. "I *say!*"

It was almost comically the old Mrs. Bridgenorth. "But I gather from her that he was bad."

"Then what was *she?*"

I barely hesitated. "What were *you?*"

"That's my own business." And she turned again to the picture. "He was good enough for her to do *that* of him."

I took it in once more. "Artistically speaking, for the way it's done, it's one of the most curious things I've ever seen."

"It's a grand treat!" said poor Mrs. Bridgenorth more simply.

It was, it *is* really; which is exactly what made the case so interesting. "Yet I feel somehow that, as I say, it wasn't done with love."

It was wonderful how she understood. "It was done with rage."

"Then what have you to fear?"

She knew again perfectly. "What happened when he made *me* jealous. So such," she declared, "that if you'll give me your word for silence—"

"Well?"

"Why, I'll double the money."

"Oh," I replied, taking a turn about in the excitement of our concurrence, "that's exactly what—to do a still better stroke for her—it had just come to *me* to propose!"

"It's understood then, on your oath, as a gentleman?" She was so eager that practically this settled it, though I moved to and fro a little while she watched me in suspense. It vibrated all round us that she had gone out to the thing in a stifled flare, that a whole close relation had in the few minutes revived. We know it of the truly amiable person that he will strain a point for another that he wouldn't strain for himself. The stroke to put in for Mary was positively prescribed. The work represented really much more than had been covenanted, and if the purchaser chose so to value it this was her own affair. I decided. "If it's understood also on *your* word."

We were so at one that we shook hands on it. "And when may I send?"

"Well, I shall see her this evening. Say early tomorrow."

"Early tomorrow." And I went with her to her brougham, into which, I remember, as she took leave, she expressed regret that she mightn't then and there have introduced the canvas for removal. I consoled her with remarking that she couldn't have got it in—which was not quite true.

I saw Mary Tredick before dinner, and though I was not quite ideally sure of my present ground with her I instantly brought out my news. "She's so delighted that I felt I must in conscience do something still better for you. She's not to have it on the original terms. I've put up the price."

Mary wondered. "But to what?"

"Well, to four hundred. If you say so, I'll try even for five."

"Oh, she'll never give that."

"I beg your pardon."

"After the agreement?" She looked grave. "I don't like such leaps and bounds."

"But, my dear child, they're yours. You contracted for a decorative trifle, and you've produced a breathing masterpiece."

She thought. "Is that what she calls it?" Then, as having to think too, I hesitated, "What does she know?" she pursued.

"She knows she wants it."

"So much as that?"

At this I had to brace myself a little. "So much that she'll send me the cheque this afternoon, and that you'll have mine by the first post in the morning."

"Before she has even received the picture?"

"Oh, she'll send for it tomorrow." And as I was dining out and had still to dress, my time was up. Mary came with me to the door, where I repeated my assurance. "You shall receive my cheque by the first post." To which I added: "If it's little enough for a Lady so much in need to pay for *any* husband, it isn't worth mentioning as the price of such a one as you've given her!"

I was in a hurry, but she held me. "Then you've felt your idea confirmed?"

"My idea?"

"That that's what I *have* given her?"

I suddenly fancied I had perhaps gone too far; but I had kept my cab and was already in it. "Well, put it," I called with excess of humour over the front, "that you've, at any rate, given *him* a wife!"

When on my return from dinner that night I let myself in, my first care, in my dusty studio, was to make light for another look at Mary's subject. I felt the impulse to bid him good night, but, to my astonishment, he was no longer there. His place was a void—he had already disappeared. I saw, however, after my first surprise, what had happened—saw it moreover, frankly, with some relief. As my servants were in bed I could ask no questions, but it was clear that Mrs. Bridgenorth, whose note, containing its cheque, lay on my table, had been after all unable to wait. The note, I found, mentioned nothing but the enclosure; but it had come by hand, and it was her silence that told the tale. Her messenger had been instructed to "act"; he had come with a vehicle, he had transferred to it canvas and frame. The prize was now therefore landed and the incident closed. I didn't altogether, the next morning, know why, but I had slept the better for the sense of these things, and as soon as my attendant came in I asked for details. It was on this that his answer surprised me. "No, sir, there was no man; she came herself. She had only a four-wheeler, but I helped her, and we got it in. It was a squeeze, sir, but she *would* take it."

I wondered. "She had a four-wheeler? and not her servant?"

"No, no, sir. She came, as you may say, single-handed."

"And not even in her brougham, which would have been larger."

My man, with his habit, weighed it. "But *have* she a brougham, sir?"

"Why, the one she was here in yesterday."

Then light broke. "Oh, *that* lady! It wasn't her, sir. It was Miss Tredick."

Light broke, but darkness a little followed it—a darkness that, after breakfast, guided my steps back to my friend. There, in its own first place, I met her creation; but I saw it would be a different thing meeting *her*. She immediately put down on a table, as if she had expected me, the cheque I had sent her overnight. "Yes, I've brought it away. And I can't take the money."

I found myself in despair. "You want to keep him?"

"I don't understand what has happened."

"You just back out?"

"I don't understand," she repeated, "what has happened." But what I had already perceived was, on the contrary, that she very nearly, that she in fact quite remarkably, did understand. It was as if in my zeal I had given away my case, and I felt that my test was coming. She had been think-ing all night with intensity, and Mrs. Bridgenorth's gen-erosity, coupled with Mrs. Bridgenorth's promptitude, had kept her awake. Thence, for a woman nervous and critical, imaginations, visions, questions. "Why, in writing me last night, did you take for granted it was *she* who had swooped down? Why," asked Mary Tredick, "should she swoop?"

"Well, if I could drive a bargain for Mary, I felt I could *a fortiori* lie for her. "Because it's her way. She does swoop. She's impatient and uncontrolled. And it's affectation for you to pretend," I said with diplomacy, "that you see no reason for her falling in love—"

"Falling in love?" She took me straight up.

"With that gentleman. Certainly. What woman wouldn't? What woman didn't? I really don't see, you know, your right to back out."

"I won't back out," she presently returned, "if you'll answer me a question. Does she know the man represented?" Then as I hung fire: "It has come to me that she must. It would account for so much. For the strange way I feel," she went on, "and for the extraordinary sum you've been able to extract from her."

It was a pity, and I flushed with it, besides wincing at the word she used. But Mrs. Bridgenorth and I, between us, had clearly made the figure too high. "You think that, if she *had* guessed, I would naturally work it to 'extract' more?"

She turned away from me on this and, looking blank in her trouble, moved vaguely about. Then she stopped. "I see him set up there. I hear her say it. What you said she would make him pass for."

I believe I foolishly tried—though only for an instant—to look as if I didn't remember what I had said. "Her husband?"

"He wasn't."

The next minute I had risked it. "Was he yours?"

I don't know what I had expected, but I found myself surprised at her mere pacific headshake. "No."

"Then why mayn't he have been——?"

"Another woman's? Because he died, to my absolute knowledge, unmarried." She spoke as quietly. "He had known many women, and there was one in particular with whom he became—and too long remained—ruinously intimate. She tried to make him marry her, and he was very near it. Death, however, saved him. But she was the reason——"

"Yes?" I feared again from her a wave of pain, and I went on while she kept it back. "Did you know her?"

"She was one I wouldn't." Then she brought it out. "She was the reason he failed me." Her successful detachment somehow said all, reduced me to a flat, kind "Oh!" that marked my sense of her telling me, against my expectation, more than I knew what to do with. But it was just while I wondered how to turn her confidence that she repeated, in a changed voice, her challenge of a moment before. "Does she know the man represented?"

"I haven't the least idea." And having so acquired myself I added, with what strikes me now as futility: "She certainly—yesterday—didn't name him."

"Only recognised him?"

"If she did she brillianty concealed it."

"So that you got nothing from her?"

It was a question that offered me a certain advantage. "I thought you accused me of getting too much."

She gave me a long look, and I now saw everything in her face. "It's very nice—what you're doing for me, and you do it handsomely. It's beautiful—beautiful, and I thank you with all my heart. But I know."

"And what do you know?"

She went about now preparing her usual work. "What he must have been to her."

"You mean she was the person?"

"Well," she said, putting on her old spectacles, "she was one of them."

"And you accept so easily the astounding coincidence—?"

"Of my finding myself, after years, in so extraordinary a relation with her? What do you call easily? I've passed a night of torment."

"But what put it into your head—?"

"That I had so blindly and strangely given him back to her? *You* put it—yesterday."

"And how?"

"I can tell you. You didn't in the least mean to—on the contrary. But you dropped the seed. The plant, after you had gone," she said with a businesslike pull at her easel, "the plant began to grow. I *saw* them there—in your studio—face to face."

"You were jealous?" I laughed.

She gave me through her glasses another look, and they seemed, from this moment, in their queerness, to have placed her quite on the other side of the gulf of time. She was firm there; she was settled; I couldn't get at her now. "I see she told you I *would* be." I doubtless kept down too little my start at it, and she immediately pursued. "You say I accept the coincidence, which is of course prodigious. But such things happen. Why shouldn't I accept it if you do?"

"*Do I?*" I smiled.

She began her work in silence, but she presently exclaimed: "I'm glad I didn't meet her!"

"I don't yet see why you wouldn't."

"Neither do I. It was an instinct."

"Your instincts"—I tried to be ironic—"are miraculous."

"They *have* to be, to meet such accidents. I must ask you kindly to tell her, when you return her gift, that now I have done the picture I find I must after all keep it for myself."

"Giving no reason?"

She painted away. "She'll know the reason."

Well, by this time I knew it too; I knew so many things that I fear my resistance was weak. If our wonderful client hadn't been his wife in fact, she was not to be helped to become his wife in fiction. I knew almost more than I can say, more at any rate than I could then betray. He had been bound in common mercy to stand by my friend, and he had basely forsaken her. This indeed brought up the obscure, into which I shyly gazed. "Why, even granting your theory, should you grudge her the portrait? It was painted in bitterness."

"Yes. Without that—!"

"It wouldn't have come? Precisely. Is it in bitterness, then, you'll keep it?"

She looked up from her canvas. "In what would *you* keep it?"

It made me jump. "Do you mean I *may*?" Then I had my idea. "I'd give you her price for it!"

Her smile through her glasses was beautiful. "And afterwards make it over to her? You shall have it when I die." With which she came away from her easel, and I saw that I was staying her work and should properly go. So I put out my hand to her. "It took—whatever you will—to paint it," she said, "but I shall keep it in joy." I could answer nothing now—had to cease to pretend; the thing was in her hands. For a moment we stood there, and I had again the sense, melancholy and final, of her being, as it were, remotely glazed and fixed into what she had done. "He's taken from me, and for all those years he's kept. Then she herself, by a prodigy—!" She lost herself again in the wonder of it.

"Unwittingly gives him back?"

She fairly, for an instant over the marvel, closed her eyes. "Gives him back."

Then it was I saw how he would be kept! But it was the end of my vision. I could only write, ruefully enough, to Mrs. Bridgenorth, whom I never met again, but of whose death—preceding by a couple of years Mary Tredick's—I happened to hear. This is an old man's tale. I have inherited the picture, in the deep beauty of which, however, darkness still lurks. No one, strange to say, has ever recognised the model, but everyone asks his name. I don't even know it.

THE POCKETBOOK GAME

* * * * * * * * *

* * * * *

by Alice Childress

Marge ..: Day's work is an education! Well, I mean workin' in different homes you learn much more than if you was steady in one place. . . . I tell you, it really keeps your mind sharp tryin', to watch for what folks will put over on you.

What? . . . No, Marge, I do not want to help shell no beans, but I'd be more than glad to stay and have supper with you, and I'll wash the dishes after. Is that all right? . . .

Who put anything over on who? . . . Oh yes! It's like this. . . . I been working for Mrs. E . . . one day a week for several months and I notice that she has some peculiar ways. Well, there was only one thing really bothered me and that was her pocketbook habit. . . . No, not those little novels. . . . I mean her purse—her handbag.

Marge, she's got a big old pocketbook with two long straps on it . . . and whenever I'd go there, she'd be propped up in a chair with her handbag double wrapped tight around her wrist, and from room to room, she'd roam with that purse hugged to her bosom . . . yes, girl! This happens every time! No, there's nobody there but me and her. . . . Marge, I couldn't say nothin' to her! It's her purse, ain't it? She can hold it if she wants to!

I held my peace for months, tryin' to figure out how I'd make my point. . . . Well, bless Bess! Today was the day! . . . Please, Marge, keep shellin' the beans so we can eat! I know you're listenin, but you listen with your ears, not your hands.... Well, anyway, I was almost ready to go home when she steps in the room hangin' onto her bag as usual and says, "Mildred, will you ask the super to come up and fix the kitchen faucet?" "Yes, Mrs. E ..." I says, "as soon as I leave." "Oh, no," she says, "he may be gone by then. Please go now." "All right," I says, and out the door I went, still wearin' my Hoover apron.

I just went down the hall and stood there a few minutes ... and then I rushed back to the door and knocked on it as hard and frantic as I could. She flung open the door sayin', "What's the matter? Did you see the super?" ... "No," I says, gaspin' hard for breath, "I was almost downstairs when I remembered ... I left my pocketbook!"

With that I dashed in, grabbed my purse and then went down to get the supper. Later, when I was leavin' she says real timid like, "Mildred, I hope that you don't think I distrust you because ..." I cut her off real quick.... "That's all right, Mrs. E ..., I understand. 'Cause if I paid anybody as little as you pay me, I'd hold my pocketbook too!"

Marge, you fool ... lookout! ... You gonna drop the beans on the floor!

ESTHER KAHN

* * * * * * * * *

by Arthur Symons

*Esther Kahn was born in one of those dark, evil-*smelling streets with strange corners which lie about the Docks. It was a quiet street, which seemed to lead nowhere, but to stand aside, for some not quite honest purpose of its own. The blinds of some of these houses were always drawn; shutters were nailed over some of the windows. Few people passed; there were never many children playing in the road; the women did not stand talking at their open doors. The doors opened and shut quietly; dark faces looked out from behind the windows; the Jews who lived there seemed always to be at work, bending over their tables, sewing and cutting, or else hurrying in and out with bundles of clothes under their arms, going and coming from the tailors for whom they worked! The Kahns all worked at tailoring: Esther's father and mother and grandmother, her elder brother and her two elder sisters. One did seaming, another button-holing, another sewed on buttons; and, on the poor pay they got for that, seven had to live.

As a child Esther had a strange terror of the street in which she lived. She was never sure whether something dreadful had just happened there, or whether it was just going to happen. But she was always in suspense. She was tormented with the fear of knowing what went on behind those nailed shutters. She made up stories about the houses, but the stories never satisfied her. She imagined some great, vague gesture; not an incident, but a gesture; and it hung in the air suspended like a shadow. The gestures of people

always meant more to her than their words; they seemed
to have a secret meaning of their own, which the words never
quite interpreted. She was always unconsciously on the
watch for their meaning.

At night, after supper, the others used to sit around the
table, talking eagerly. Esther would get up and draw her
chair into the corner by the door, and for a time she would
watch them, as if she were looking on at something, something with which she had no concern, but which interested
her for its outline and movement. She saw her father's keen
profile, the great nose, the black prominent eyes, the tangled
black hair straggling over the shirt-collar; her mother, large,
placid, with masses of black, straight hair coiled low over
her sallow cheeks; the two sisters, sharp and voluble, never
at rest for a moment; the brother, with his air of insolent
assurance, an immense self-satisfaction hooded under his
beautifully curved eyelids; the grandmother, with her bent
and mountainous shoulders, the vivid malice of her eyes,
her hundreds of wrinkles. All these people, who had so many
interests in common, who thought of the same things, cared
for the same things, seemed so fond of one another in an
instinctive way, with so much hostility for other people who
were not belonging to them, sat there night after night, in
the same attitudes, always as eager for the events of today
as they had been for the events of yesterday. Everything
mattered to them immensely, and especially their part in
things; and no one thing seemed to matter more than any
other thing. Esther cared only to look on; nothing mattered
to her; she had no interest in their interests; she was not
sure that she cared for them more than she would care for
other people; they were what she supposed real life was,
that was a thing in which she had only a disinterested curiosity.

Sometimes, when she had been watching them until they had all seemed to fade away and form again in a kind of vision more precise than the reality, she would lose sight of them altogether and sit gazing straight before her, her eyes wide open, her lips parted. Her hands would make an unconscious movement, as if she were accompanying some grave words with an appropriate gesture, and Becky would generally see it, and burst into a mocking laugh, and ask her whom she was mimicking.

"Don't notice her," the mother said once; "she's not a human child, she's a monkey; she's clutching out after a soul, as they do. They look like little men, but they know they're not men, and they try to be; that's why they mimic us."

Esther was very angry; she said to herself that she would be more careful in future not to show anything that she was feeling.

At thirteen Esther looked a woman. She was large-boned, with very small hands and feet, and her body seemed to be generally asleep, in a kind of brooding lethargy. She had her mother's hair, masses of it, but softer, with a faint natural wave in it. Her face was oval, smooth in outline. The lips were red, strung like a bow. The whole face seemed to await, with an infinite patience, some moulding and awakening force, which might have its way with it. It wanted nothing, anticipated nothing; it waited. Only the eyes put life into the mask, and the eyes were the eyes of the tribe; they had no personal meaning in what seemed to be their mystery; they were ready to fascinate innocently, to be intolerably ambiguous without intention; they were fathomless with mere sleep, the unconscious dream which is in the eyes of animals.

Esther was neither clever nor stupid; she was inert. She did as little in the house as she could, but when she had to take her share in the stitching she stitched more neatly than any of the others, though very slowly. She hated it, in her languid smouldering way, partly because it was work and partly because it made her prick her fingers, and the skin grew hard and ragged where the point of the needle had scratched it. She liked her skin to be quite smooth, but all the glycerine she rubbed into it at night would not take out the mark of the needle. It seemed to her like the badge of her slavery.

She would rather not have been a Jew; that, too, was a kind of badge, marking her out from other people; she wanted to be let alone, to have her own way without other people's help or hindrance. She had no definite consciousness of what her own way was to be; she was only conscious, as yet, of the ways that would certainly not be hers.

She would not think only of making money, like her mother, nor of being thought clever, like Becky, nor of being admired because she had good looks and dressed smartly, like Mina. All these things required an effort, and Esther was lazy. She wanted to be admired, and to have money, of course, and she did not want people to think her stupid; but all this was to come to her, she knew, because of some fortunate quality in herself, as yet undiscovered. Then she would shake off everything that now clung to her, like a worn-out garment that one keeps only until one can replace it. She saw herself rolling away in a carriage towards the west; she would never come back. And it would be like a revenge on whatever it was that kept her stifling in this mean street; she wanted to be cruelly revenged.

As it was, her only very keen pleasure was in going to the

theatre with her brother or her sisters; she cared nothing
for music-halls, and preferred staying at home to going with
the others when they went to the Pavilion or the Foresters.
But when there was a melodrama at the Standard, or at the
Elephant and Castle, she would wait and struggle outside
the door and up the narrow, winding stairs, for a place as
near the front of the gallery as she could get. Once inside,
she would never speak, but she would sit staring at the
people on the stage as if they hypnotised her. She never
criticised the play, as the others did; the play did not seem
to matter; she lived in it without will or choice, merely because it was there and her eyes were on it.

But after it was over and they were at home again, she
would become suddenly voluble as she discussed the merits
of the acting. She had no hesitations, was certain that she
was always in the right, and became furious if anyone
contradicted her. She saw each part as a whole, and she
blamed the actors for not being consistent with themselves.
She could not understand how they could make a mistake.
It was so simple, there were no two ways of doing anything.
To go wrong was as if you said no when you meant yes;
it must be wilful.

"You ought to do it yourself, Esther," said her sisters,
when they were tired of her criticisms. They meant to be
satirical, but Esther said, seriously enough: "Yes, I could
do it; but so could that woman if she would let herself alone.
Why did she try to be something else all the time?"

Time went slowly with Esther; but when she was seventeen she was still sewing at home and still waiting. Nothing
had come to her of all that she had expected. Two of her
cousins, and a neighbour or two, had wanted to marry her;
but she had refused them contemptuously. To her sluggish

instinct men seemed only good for making money, or, perhaps, children; they had not come to have any definite personal meaning for her. A little man called Joel, who had
talked to her passionately about love, and had cried when
she refused him, seemed to her an unintelligible and ridiculous kind of animal. When she dreamed of the future, there
was never anyone of that sort making fine speeches to her.

But, gradually, her own real purpose in life had become
clear. She was to be an actress. She said nothing about it at
home, but she began to go round to the managers of the
small theatres in the neighbourhood, asking for an engagement. After a long time the manager gave her a small part.
The piece was called "The Wages of Sin." and she was to
be the servant, who opens the door in the first act to the
man who is going to be the murderer in the second act, and
then identifies him in the fourth act.

Esther went home quietly and said nothing until supper-
time. Then she said to her mother: "I am going on the
stage."

"That's very likely," said her mother, with a sarcastic
smile, "and when do you go on, pray?"

"On Monday night," said Esther.

"You don't mean it!" said her mother.

"Indeed I mean it," said Esther, "and I've got my part.
I'm to be the servant in 'The Wages of Sin.' "

Her brother laughed. "I know," he said, "she speaks two
words twice."

"You are right," said Esther; "will you come on Monday,
and hear how I say them?"

When Esther had made up her mind to do anything, they
all knew that she always did it. Her father talked to her
seriously. Her mother said: "You are much too lazy, Esther;

* * * *

you will never get on." They told her that she was taking the bread out of their mouths, and it was certain she would never put it back again. "If I get on," said Esther, "I will pay you back exactly what I would have earned, as long as you keep me. Is that a bargain? I know I shall get on, and you won't repent of it. You had better let me do as I want. It will pay."

They shook their heads, looked at Esther, who sat there with her lips tight shut, and a queer, hard look in her eyes, which were trying not to seem exultant; they looked at one another, shook their heads again, and consented. The old grandmother mumbled something fiercely, but as it sounded like bad words, and they never knew what Old Testament language she would use, they did not ask her what she was meaning.

On Monday Esther made her first appearance on the stage. Her mother said to her afterwards: "I thought nothing of you, Esther; you were just like any ordinary servant." Becky asked her if she had felt nervous. She shook her head; it had seemed quite natural to her, she said. She did not tell them that a great wave of triumph had swept over her as she felt the heat of the gas footlights come up into her eyes, and saw the floating cluster of white faces rising out of a solid mass of indistinguishable darkness. In that moment she drew into her nostrils the breath of life.

Esther had a small part to understudy, and before long she had the chance of playing it. The manager said nothing to her, but soon afterwards he told her to understudy a more important part. She never had the chance to play it, but, when the next piece was put on at the theatre, she was given a part of her own. She began to make a little money, and, as she had promised, she paid so much a week to her parents for keeping her. They gained by the bargain, so they did

not ask her to come back to the stitching. Mrs. Kahn sometimes spoke of her daughter to the neighbours with a certain
languid pride; Esther was making her way.

Esther made her way rapidly. One day the manager of a
West End theatre came down to see her; he engaged her at
once to play a small, but difficult part in an ambitious kind
of melodrama that he was bringing out. She did it well,
satisfied the manager, was given a better part, did that
well, too, was engaged by another manager, and, in short,
began to be looked upon as a promising actress. The papers
praised her with moderation; some of the younger critics,
who admired her type, praised her more than she deserved.
She was making money; she had come to live in rooms of
her own, off the Strand; at twenty-one she had done, in a
measure what she wanted to do; but she was not satisfied
with herself. She had always known that she could act, but
how well could she act? Would she never be able to act any
better than this? She had drifted into the life of the stage
as naturally as if she had never known anything else; she
was at home, comfortable, able to do what many others could
not do. But she wanted to be a great actress.

An old actor, Nathan Quellen, who had taken a kind
of paternal interest in her, and who helped her with all the
good advice that he had never taken to himself, was fond of
saying that the remedy was in her own hands.

"My dear Esther," he would tell her, smoothing his long
grey hair down over his forehead, "you must take a lover;
you must fall in love; there's no other way. You think you
can act, and you have never felt anything worse than a cut
finger. Why it's an absurdity! Wait till you know the only
thing worth knowing; till then you're in short frocks and
a pinafore."

He cited examples, he condensed the biographies of the

great actresses for her benefit. He found one lesson in them all, and he was sincere in his reading of history as he saw it. He talked, argued, protested; the matter seriously troubled him. He felt he was giving Esther good advice; he wanted her to be the thing she wanted to be. Esther knew it and thanked him, without smiling; she sat brooding over his words; she never argued against them. She believed much of what he said; but was the remedy, as he said, in her own hands? It did not seem so.

As yet no man had spoken to her blood. She had the sluggish blood of a really profound animal nature. She saw men calmly, as calmly as when little Joel had cried because she would not marry him. Joel still came to see her sometimes, with the same entreaty in his eyes, not daring to speak it. Other men, very different men, had made love to her in very different ways. They had seemed to be trying to drive a hard bargain, to get the better of her in a matter of business; and her native cunning had kept her easily on the better side of the bargain. She was resolved to be a business woman in the old trade of the affections; no one should buy or sell her except at her own price, and she set the price vastly high.

Yet Quellen's words set her thinking. Was there, after all, but one way to study for the stage? All the examples pointed to it, and, what was worse, she felt it might be true. She saw exactly where her acting stopped short.

She looked around her with practical eyes, not seeming to herself to be doing anything unusual or unlikely to succeed in its purpose. She thought deliberately over all the men she knew; but who was there whom it would be possible to take seriously? She could think of only one man: Philip Haygarth.

Philip Haygarth was a man of five-and-thirty, who had been writing plays and having them acted, with only a moderate success for nearly ten years. He was one of the accepted men, a man whose plays were treated respectfully, and he had the reputation of being much cleverer than his plays. He was short, dark, neat, very worldly looking, with thin lips and reflective, not quite honest eyes. His manner was cold, restrained, with a mingling of insolence and diffidence. He was a hard worker and a somewhat deliberately hard liver. He avoided society and preferred to find his relaxation among people with whom one did not need to keep up appearances, or talk sentiment, or pay afternoon calls. He admired Esther Kahn as an actress, though with many reservations; and he admired her as a woman, more than he ever admired anybody else. She appealed to all his tastes; she ended by absorbing almost the whole of those interests and those hours which he set apart, in his carefully arranged life, for such matters.

He made love to Esther much more skilfully than any of her other lovers, and, though she saw through his plans as clearly as he wished her to see through them, she was grateful to him for a certain finesse in his manner of approach. He never mentioned the word "love," except to jest at it; he concealed even the extent to which he was really disturbed by her presence; his words spoke only of friendship and of general topics. And yet there could never be any doubt as to his meaning; his whole attitude was a patient waiting. He interested her; frankly, he interested her: here, then, was the man for her purpose. With his admirable tact, he spared her the least difficulty in making her meaning clear. He congratulated himself on a prize; she congratulated herself on the accomplishment of a duty.

Days and weeks passed, and Esther scrutinised herself
with a distinct sense of disappointment. She had no moral
feeling in the matter; she was her own property, it has always seemed to her, free to dispose of as she pleased. The
business element in her nature persisted. This bargain, this
infinitely important bargain, had been concluded, with open
eyes, with a full sense of responsibility, for a purpose, the
purpose for which she lived. What was the result?

She could see no result. The world had in no sense
changed for her, as she had been supposing it would change;
a new excitement had come into her life, and that was all.
She wondered what it was that a woman was expected to feel
under the circumstances, and why she had not felt it. How
different had been her feelings when she walked across the
stage for the first time! That had really been a new life, or
the very beginning of life. But this was no more than a
delightful episode, hardly to be disentangled from the visit
to Paris which had accompanied it. She had, so to speak,
fallen into a new habit, which was so agreeable, and seemed
so natural, that she could not understand why she had not
fallen into it before; it was a habit she would certainly per-
sist in, for its own sake. The world remained just the same.

And her art: she had learned nothing. No new thrill came
into the words she spoke; her eyes, as they looked across
the footlights, remembered nothing, had nothing new to tell.

And so she turned, with all the more interest, an interest
almost impersonal, to Philip Haygarth when he talked to
her about acting and the drama, when he elaborated his
theories which, she was aware, occupied him more than she
occupied him. He was one of those creative critics who can
do every man's work but their own. When he sat down to
write his own plays, something dry and hard came into the

words, the life ebbed out of those imaginary people who had
been so real to him, whom he had made so real to others
as he talked. He constructed admirably and was an unerring
judge of the construction of plays. And he had a sense of
acting which was like the sense that a fine actor might have,
if he could be himself and also someone looking on at himself. He not only knew what should be done, but exactly why
it should be done. Little suspecting that he had been chosen
for the purpose, though in so different a manner, he set
himself to teach her art to Esther.

He made her go through the great parts with him; she was
Juliet, Lady Macbeth, Cleopatra; he taught her how to
speak verse and how to feel the accent of speech in verse,
another kind of speech than prose speech, he trained her
voice to take hold of the harmonies that lie in words themselves; and she caught them, by ear, as one born to speak
many languages catches a foreign language. She went
through Ibsen as she had gone through Shakespeare; and
Haygarth showed her how to take hold of this very difficult
subject-matter, so definite and so elusive. And they studied
good acting-plays together, worthless plays that gave the
actress opportunities to create something out of nothing.
Together they saw Duse and Sarah Bernhardt; and they
had seen Réjane in Paris, in crudely tragic parts; and they
studied the English stage, to find out why it maintained itself
at so stiff a distance from nature. She went on acting all the
time, always acting with more certainty; and at last she
attempted more serious parts, which she learned with
Haygarth at her elbow.

She had to be taught her part as a child is taught its lesson; word by word, intonation by intonation. She read it
over, not really knowing what it was about; she learned it

by heart mechanically, getting the words into her memory first. Then the meaning had to be explained to her, scene by scene, and she had to say the words over until she had found the right accent. Once found, she never forgot it; she could repeat it identically at any moment; there were no variations to allow for. Until that moment she was reaching out blindly in the dark, feeling about her with uncertain fingers.

And, with her, the understanding came with the power of expression, sometimes seeming really to proceed from the sound to the sense, from the gesture inward. Show her how it should be done, and she knew why it should be done; sound the right notes in her ears, arrest her at the moment when the note came right, and she understood, by a backward process, why the note should sound thus. Her mind worked, but it worked under suggestion, as the hypnotists say; the idea had to come to her through the instinct, or it would never come.

As Esther found herself, almost unconsciously, becoming what she had dreamed of becoming, what she had longed to become, and, after all, through Philip Haygarth, a more personal feeling began to grow up in her heart towards this lover who had found his way to her, not through the senses, but through the mind. A kind of domesticity had crept into their relations, and this drew Esther nearer to him. She began to feel that he belonged to her. He had never, she knew, been wholly absorbed in her, and she had delighted him by showing no jealousy, no anxiety to keep him. As long as she remained so, he felt that she had a sure hold on him. But now she began to change, to concern herself more with his doings, to assert her right to him, as she had never hitherto cared to do. He chafed a little at what seemed an unnecessary devotion.

Love, with Esther, had come slowly, taking his time on the journey; but he came to take possession. To work at her art was to please Philip Haygarth; she worked now with a double purpose. And she made surprising advances as an actress. People began to speculate: had she genius, or was this only an astonishingly developed talent, which could go so far and no farther?

For, in this finished method, which seemed so spontaneous and yet at the same time so deliberate, there seemed still to be something, some slight, essential, almost unaccountably lacking. What was it? Was it a fundamental lack, that could never be supplied? Or would that slight, essential thing, as her admirers prophesied, one day be supplied? They waited.

Esther was now really happy, for the first time in her life; and as she looked back over those years, in the street by the Docks, when she had lived alone in the midst of her family, and since then, when she had lived alone, working, not finding the time long, nor wishing it to go more slowly, she felt a kind a surprise at herself. How could she have gone through it all? She had not ever been bored. She had had a purpose, and now that she was achieving that purpose, the thing itself seemed hardly to matter. Her art kept pace with her life: she was giving up nothing in return for happiness; but she had come to prize the happiness, her love, beyond all things.

She knew that Haygarth was proud of her, that he looked upon her talent, genius, whatever it was, as partly the work of his hands. It pleased her that this should be so; it seemed to bind him to her more tightly.

In this she was mistaken, as most women are mistaken when they ask themselves what it is in them that holds their lovers. The actress interested Haygarth greatly, but the actress interested him as a problem, as something quite apart from his feelings as a man, as a lover. He had been attracted

by the woman, by what was sombre and unexplained in
her eyes, by the sleepy grace of her movements, by the
magnetism that seemed to drowse in her. He had made love
to her precisely as he would have made love to an ignorant,
beautiful creature who walked on in some corner of a
Drury Lane melodrama. On principle, he did not like clever
women. Esther, it is true, was not clever, in the ordinary,
tiresome sense; and her startling intuition, in matters of
acting, had not repelled him, as an exhibition of the capa-
bilities of woman, while they preoccupied him for a long
time in that part of his brain which worked critically upon
any interesting material. But nothing that she could do as an
artist made the least difference to his feeling about her as a
woman; his pride in her was like his pride in a play that he
had written finely, and put aside; to be glanced at from time
to time, with cool satisfaction. He had his own very deliberate theory of values, and one value was never allowed to
interfere with another. A devoted, discreet amateur of
woman, he appreciated women really for their own sakes,
with an unflattering simplicity. And for a time Esther
absorbed him almost wholly.

He had been quite content with their relations as they
were before she fell seriously in love with him, and this new,
profound feeling, which he had never even dreaded, somewhat disturbed him. She was adopting almost the attitude
of a wife, and he had no ambition to play the part of a husband. The affections were always rather a strain upon him;
he liked something a little less serious and a little more
exciting.

Esther understood nothing that was going on in Philip
Haygarth's mind, and when he began to seem colder to her,
when she saw less of him, and then less, it seemed to her that

she could still appeal to him by art and still touch him by her devotion. As her warmth seemed more and more to threaten his liberty, the impulse to tug at his chain became harder to resist. He continued, unvarying interest in her acting, his patience to helping her, in working with her, kept for some time from realising how little was left now of the more personal feeling. It was a sharp surprise, as well as with a blinding rage, that she discovered one day, beyond possibility of mistake, that she had a rival, and that Haygarth was only doling out to her the time left over from her rival.

It was an Italian, a young girl who had come over to London with an organ grinder, and who posed for sculptors when she could get a sitting. It was a girl who could barely read and write, an insignificant creature, a peasant from the Campagan, who had nothing but her good looks and the distinction of her attitude. Esther was beside herself with rage, jealousy, mortification; she loved, and she could not pardon. There was a scene of unmeasured violence. Haygarth was cruel, almost with intention, and they parted, Esther feeling as if her life had been broken sharply in two.

She was at the last rehearsals of a new play by Haygarth, a play in which he had tried for once to be tragic in the bare straightforward way of the things that really happened. She went through the rehearsals absentmindedly, repeating her words, which he had taught her how to say, but scarcely attending to their meaning. Another thought was at work behind this mechanical speech, a continual throb of remembrance, going on monotonously. Her mind was full of other words, which she heard as if an inner voice were repeating them; her mind made up pictures, which seemed to pass slowly before her eyes: Haygarth and the other woman. At the last rehearsal Quellen came round to her, and, ironically as she thought, complimented her on her performance. She meant, when the night came, not to fail: that was all.

When the night came, she said to herself that she was calm, that she would be able to concentrate herself on her acting and act just as usual But, as she stood in the wings, waiting for her moment to appear, her eyes went straight to the eyes of the other woman, the Italian model, the organ-grinder's girl, who sat smiling contently, in the front of a box, turning her head sometimes to speak to someone behind her, hidden by the curtain. She was dressed in black, with a rose in her hair: you could have taken her for a lady: she was triumphantly beautiful. Esther shuddered as if she had been struck; the blood rushed into her forehead and swelled and beat against her eyes. Then, with an immense effort, she cleared her mind of everything but the task before her. Every nerve in her body lived with a separate life as she opened the door at the back of the stage, and stood waiting for the applause to subside, motionless under the eyes of the audience. There was something in the manner of her entrance that seemed to strike the fatal note of the play. She had never been more restrained, more effortless; she seemed scarcely to be acting; only, a magnetic current seemed to have been set in motion between her and those who were watching her. They held their breaths, as if they were assisting at a real tragedy; as if, at any moment, this acting might give place to some horrible, naked passion of mere nature. The curtain rose and rose again at the end of the first act; and she stood there, bowing gravely, in what seemed a deliberate continuation, into that interval, of the sentiment of the piece. Her dresses were taken off her and put on her, for each act, as if she had been a lay-figure. Once, in the second act, she looked up at the box; the Italian woman was smiling emptily, but Haygarth, taking no notice of her, leaned forward with his eyes fixed on the stage. After the third act he sent to Esther's dressing-room a fervent note, begging to be allowed to see her. She had made his play, he said, and she had made herself a great actress. She crumpled the note fiercely, put it carefully into her jewel box, and refused to see him. In the last act she had to die, after the manner of the Lady of the Camellias, waiting for the lover who, in this case, never came. The pathos of her acting was almost unbearable, and still, it seemed not like acting at all. The curtain went down on a great actress.

Esther went home stunned, only partly realising what she had done, or how she had done it. She read over the note from Haygarth, unforgivingly; and the long letter that came from him in the morning. As reflection returned, through all the confused suffering and excitement, to her deliberate, automatic nature, in which a great shock had brought about a kind of release, she realised that all she had wanted, during most of her life, had at last come about. The note had been struck, she had responded to it, as she responded to every suggestion, faultlessly; she knew that she could repeat the note, whenever she wished, now that she had once found it. There would be no variation to allow for, the actress was made at last. She might take back her lover, or never see him again, it would make no difference. It would make no difference, she repeated, over and over again, weeping uncontrollable tears.

MANNEQUIN

* * * * * * *

* * *

by Jean Rhys

Twelve o'clock. Déjeuner chez Jeanne Veron, Place Vendôme.

Anna, dressed in the black cotton, chemiselike garment of the mannequin off duty was trying to find her way along dark passages and down complicated flights of stairs to the underground room where lunch was served.

She was shivering, for she had forgotten her coat, and the garment that she wore was very short, sleeveless, displaying her rose-coloured stockings to the knee. Her hair was flamingly and honestly red; her eyes, which were very gentle in expression, brown and heavily shadowed with kohl; her face small and pale under its professional rouge. She was fragile, like a delicate child, her arms pathetically thin. It was to her legs that she owed this dazzling, this incredible opportunity.

Madame Veron, white-haired with black eyes incredibly distinguished, who had given them one sweeping glance, the glance of the connoisseur, smiled imperiously and engaged her at an exceedingly small salary. As a beginner, Madame explained, Anna could not expect more. She was to wear the jeune fillé dresses. Another smile, another sharp glance.

Anna was conducted from the Presence by an underling who helped her to take off the frock she had worn temporarily for the interview. Aspirants for an engagement are always dressed in a model of the house.

She had spent yesterday afternoon in a delirium tempered

by a feeling of exaggerated reality, and in buying the necessary make up. It had been such a forlorn hope, answering the advertisement.

The morning had been dreamlike. At the back of the wonderfully decorated salons she had found an unexpected sombreness; the place, empty, would have been dingy and melancholy, countless puzzling corridors and staircases, a rabbit warren and a labyrinth. She despaired of ever finding her way.

In the mannequins' dressing-room she spent a shy hour making up her face—in an extraordinary and distinctive atmosphere of slimness and beauty; white arms and faces vivid with rouge; raucous voices and the smell of cosmetics; silken lingerie. Coldly critical glances were bestowed upon Anna's reflection in the glass. None of them looked at her directly. . . . A depressing room, taken by itself, bare and cold, a very inadequate conservatory for these human flowers. Saleswomen in black rushed in and out, talking in sharp voices; a very old woman hovered, helpless and shapeless, showing Anna where to hang her clothes, presenting to her the black garment that Anna was wearing, going to lunch. She smiled with professional motherliness, her little, sharp, black eyes travelling rapidly from la nouvelle's hair to her ankles and back again.

She was Madame Pecard, the dresser.

Before Anna had spoken a word she was called away by a small boy in buttons to her destination in one of the salons: there, under the eye of a vendeuse, she had to learn the way to wear the innocent and springlike air and garb of the jeune fille. Behind a yellow, silken screen she was hustled into a leather coat and paraded under the cold eyes of an American buyer. This was the week when the spring models are shown to important people from big shops all over Europe and America: the most critical week of the season.... The American buyer said that he would have that, but with an inch on to the collar and larger cuffs. In vain the saleswoman, in her best English with its odd Chicago accent, protested that that would completely ruin the chic of the model. The American buyer knew what he wanted and saw that he got it.

The vendeuse sighed, but there was a note of admiration in her voice. She respected Americans: they were not like the English, who, under a surface of annoying moroseness of manner, were notoriously timid and easy to turn round your finger.

"Was that all right?" Behind the screen one of the saleswomen smiled encouragingly and nodded. The other shrugged her shoulders. She had small, close-set eyes, a long thin nose and tight lips of the regulation puce colour. Behind her silken screen Anna sat on a high white stool. She felt that she appeared charming and troubled. The white and gold of the salon suited her red hair.

A short morning. For the mannequin's day begins at ten and the process of making up lasts an hour. The friendly saleswoman volunteered the information that her name was Jeannine, that she was in the lingerie, that she considered Anna rudement jolie, that noon was Anna's lunch hour. She must go down the corridor and up those stairs, through the big salon then.... Anyone would tell her. But Anna, lost in the labyrinth, was too shy to ask her way. Besides, she was not sorry to have time to brace herself for the ordeal. She had reached the regions of utility and oilcloth: the decorative salons were far overhead. Then the smell of food—almost visible, it was so cloudlike and heavy—came to her nostrils, and high-noted, and sibilant, a buzz of conversation made her draw a deep breath. She pushed a door open.

She was in a big, very low-ceilinged room, all the floor space occupied by long wooden tables with no cloths.... She was sitting at the mannequins' table, gazing at a thick and hideous white china plate, a twisted tin fork, a wooden handled stained knife, a tumbler so thick it seemed unbreakable.

There were twelve mannequins at Jeanne Veron's: six of them were lunching, the others still paraded, goddess-like, till their turn came for rest and refreshment. Each of the twelve was of a distinct and separate type: each of the twelve knew her type and kept to it, practising rigidly in clothing, manner, voice and conversation.

Round the austere table were now seated: Babette, the gamine, the traditional blonde enfant: Mona, tall and darkly beautiful, the femme fatale, the wearer of sumptuous evening gowns. Georgette was the garçonne: Simone with green eyes Anna knew instantly for a cat whom men would and did adore, a sleek, white, purring, long-lashed creature.... Eliane was the star of the collection.

Eliane was frankly ugly and it did not matter: no doubt Lilith, from whom she was obviously descended, had been ugly too. Her hair was henna-tinted, her eyes small and black, her complexion bad under her thick make-up. Her lips were extraordinarily slim, her hands and feet exquisite, every movement she made was as graceful as a flower's in the wind. Her walk ... But it was her walk which made her the star there and earned her a salary quite fabulous for Madame Veron's, where large salaries were not the rule.... Her walk and her "chic of the devil" which lit an expression of admiration in even the cold eyes of American buyers.

Eliane was a quiet girl, pleasant-mannered. She wore a ring with a beautiful emerald on one long, slim finger, and in her small eyes were both intelligence and mystery.

Madame Pecard, the dresser, was seated at the head of the mannequins' table, talking loudly, unlistened to, and gazing benevolently at her flock.

At other tables sat the sewing girls, pale-faced, black-frocked—the workers, heroically gay, but with the stamp of labour on them: and the saleswomen. The mannequins, with their sensual, blatant charms and their painted faces were watched covertly, envied and apart.

Babette the blonde enfant was next to Anna, and having started the conversation with a few good, round oaths at the quality of the sardines, announced proudly that she could speak English and knew London very well. She began to tell Anna the history of her adventures in the city of coldness, dark and fogs. . . . She had gone to a job as a mannequin in Bond Street and the villainous proprietor of the shop having tried to make love to her and she being rigidly virtuous, she had left. And another job, Anna must figure to herself, had been impossible to get, for she, Babette, was too small and slim for the Anglo-Saxon idea of a mannequin.

She stopped to shout in a loud voice to the woman who was serving: "Hé, my old one, don't forget your little Babette. . . ."

Opposite Simone the cat and the sportive Georgette were having a low-voiced conversation about the tristeness of a monsieur of their acquaintance. "I said to him," Georgette finished decisively, "Nothing to be done, my rabbit. You have not looked at me well, little one. In my place would you not have done the same?"

She broke off when she realized that the others were listening, and smiled in a friendly way at Anna.

She too, it appeared, had ambitions to go to London because the salaries were so much better there. Was it difficult? Did they really like French girls? Parisiennes?

The conversation became general.

"The English boys are nice," said Babette, winking one divinely candid eye. "I had a chic type who used to take me to dinner at the Empire Palace. Oh, a pretty boy...."

"It is the most chic restaurant in London," she added importantly.

The meal reached the stage of dessert. The other tables were gradually emptying; the mannequins all ordered very strong coffee, several a liqueur. Only Mona and Eliane remained silent; Eliane, because she was thinking of something else; Mona because it was her type, her genre to be haughty.

Her hair swept away from her white, narrow forehead and her small ears: her long earrings nearly touching her shoulders, she sipped her coffee with a disdainful air. Only once, when the blonde enfant, having engaged in a passage of arms with the waitress and got the worst of it was momentarily discomfited and silent, Mona narrowed her eyes and smiled an astonishingly cruel smile.

As soon as her coffee was drunk she got up and went out.

Anna produced a cigarette, and Georgette, perceiving instantly that here was the sportive touch, her genre, asked for one and lit it with a devil-may-care air. Anna eagerly passed her cigarettes round, but the Mère Pecard interfered weightily. It was against the rules of the house for the mannequins to smoke, she wheezed. The girls all lit their cigarettes and smoked. The Mère Pecard rumbled on: "A caprice, my children. All the world knows that mannequins are capricious. Is it not so?" She appealed to the rest of the room.

As they went out Babette put her arm round Anna's waist and whispered: "Don't answer Madame Pecard. We don't like her. We never talk to her. She spies on us. She is a camel."

That afternoon Anna stood for an hour to have a dress draped on her. She showed this dress to a stout Dutch lady buying for the Hague, to a beautiful South American with pearls, to a silver-haired American gentleman who wanted an evening cape for his daughter of seventeen, and to a hook-nosed odd English lady of title who had a loud voice and dressed, under her furs, in a grey jersey and stout boots.

The American gentleman approved of Anna, and said so, and Anna gave him a passionately grateful glance. For, if the vendeuse Jeannine had been uniformly kind and encouraging, the other, Madame Tienne, had been as uniformly disapproving and had once even pinched her arm hard.

About five o'clock Anna became exhausted. The four white and gold walls seemed to close in on her. She sat on her high white stool staring at a marvellous nightgown and fighting an intense desire to rush away. Anywhere! Just to dress and rush away anywhere, from the raking eyes of the customers and the pinching fingers of Irene.

"I will one day. I can't stick it," she said to herself. "I won't be able to stick it." She had an absurd wish to gasp for air.

Jeannine came and found her like that.

"It is hard at first, hein? . . . One asks oneself: Why? For what good? It is all idiot. We are all so. But we go on. Do not worry about Irene." She whispered: "Madame Veron likes you very much. I heard her say so."

At six o'clock Anna was out in the rue de la Paix; her
fatigue forgotten, the feeling that now she really belonged
to the great, maddening city possessed her and she was
happy in her beautifully cut tailor-made and a beret.

Georgette passed her and smiled; Babette was in a fur
coat.

All up the street the mannequins were coming out of
the shops, pausing on the pavements a moment, making them
as gay and as beautiful as beds of flowers before they walked
swiftly away and the Paris night swallowed them up.

THE SINGING LESSON

* * * * * * * * *

* * *

by Katherine Mansfield

With despair—cold, sharp despair—buried deep in her heart like a wicked knife, Miss Meadows, in cap and gown and carrying a little baton, trod the cold corridors that led to the music hall. Girls of all ages, rosy from the air, and bubbling over with that gleeful excitement that comes from running to school on a fine autumn morning, hurried, skipped, fluttered by; from the hollow classrooms came a quick drumming of voices; a bell rang; a voice like a bird cried, "Muriel." And then there came from the staircase a tremendous knock-knock-knocking. Some one had dropped her dumbbells.

The Science Mistress stopped Miss Meadows.

"Good mor-ning," she cried, in her sweet, affected drawl. "Isn't it cold? It might be win-ter."

Miss Meadows, hugging the knife, stared in hatred at the Science Mistress. Everything about her was sweet, pale, like honey. You would not have been surprised to see a bee caught in the tangles of that yellow hair.

"It is rather sharp," said Miss Meadows, grimly.

The other smiled her sugary smile.

"You look fro-zen," said she. Her blue eyes opened wide; there came a mocking light in them. (Had she noticed anything?)

"Oh, not quite as bad as that," said Miss Meadows, and she gave the Science Mistress, in exchange for her smile, a quick grimace and passed on. . . .

Forms Four, Five, and Six were assembled in the music hall. The noise was deafening. On the platform, by the piano, stood Mary Beazley, Miss Meadows' favourite, who played accompaniments. She was turning the music stool. When she saw Miss Meadows she gave a loud, warning "Sh-sh! girls!" and Miss Meadows, her hands thrust in her sleeves, the baton under her arm, strode down the centre aisle, mounted the steps, turned sharply, seized the brass music stand, planted it in front of her, and gave two sharp taps with her baton for silence.

"Silence, please! Immediately!" and, looking at nobody, her glance swept over that sea of coloured flannel blouses, with bobbing pink faces and hands, quivering butterfly hair-bows, and music-books outspread. She knew perfectly well what they were thinking. "Meady is in a wax." Well, let them think it! Her eyelids quivered; she tossed her head, defying them. What could the thoughts of those creatures matter to some one who stood there bleeding to death, pierced to the heart, to the heart, by such a letter—

... "I feel more and more strongly that our marriage would be a mistake. Not that I do not love you. I love you as much as it is possible for me to love any woman, but, truth to tell, I have come to the conclusion that I am not a marrying man, and the idea of settling down fills me with nothing but—" and the word "disgust" was scratched out lightly and "regret" written over the top.

Basil! Miss Meadows stalked over to the piano. And Mary Beazley, who was waiting for this moment, bent forward; her curls fell over her cheeks while she breathed, "Good morning, Miss Meadows," and she motioned towards rather than handed to her mistress a beautiful yellow chrysanthemum. This little ritual of the flower had been gone through for ages and ages, quite a term and a half. It was as much part of the lesson as opening the piano. But this morning, instead of taking it up, instead of tucking it into her belt while she leant over Mary and said, "Thank you, Mary. How very nice! Turn to page thirty-two," what was Mary's horror when Miss Meadows totally ignored the chrysanthemum, made no reply to her greeting, but said in a voice of ice, "Page foureen, please, and mark the accents well."

Staggering moment! Mary blushed until the tears stood in her eyes, but Miss Meadows was gone back to the music stand; her voice rang through the music hall.

"Page fourteen. We will begin with page fourteen. 'A Lament.' Now, girls, you ought to know it by this time. We shall take it all together; not in parts, all together. And without expression. Sing it, though, quite simply, beating time with the left hand."

She raised the baton; she tapped the music stand twice. Down came Mary on the opening chord; down came all those left hands, beating the air, and in chimed those young, mournful voices:

Fast! Ah, too Fast Fade the Ro-o-ses of Pleasure;
Soon Autumn yields unto Wi-i-nter Drear.
Fleetly! Ah, Fleetly Mu-u-sic's Gay Measure
Passes away from the Listening Ear.

Good Heavens, what could be more tragic than that lament! Every note was a sigh, a sob, a groan of awful mournfulness. Miss Meadows lifted her arms in the wide gown and began conducting with both hands. "... I feel more and more strongly that our marriage would be a mistake. . . ." she beat. And the voices cried: *Fleetly!Ah,*

Fleetly. What could have possessed him to write such a letter! What could have led up to it! It came out of nothing. His last letter had been all about a fumed-oak bookcase he had bought for "our" books, and a "natty little hall-stand" he had seen, "a very neat affair with a carved owl on a bracket, holding three hat-brushes in its claws." How she had smiled at that! So like a man to think one needed three hat-brushes! *From the Listening Ear,* sang the voices.

"Once again," said Miss Meadows. "But this time in parts. Still without expression." *Fast! Ah, too Fast.* With the gloom of the contraltos added, one could scarcely help shuddering. *Fade the Roses of Pleasure.* Last time he had come to see her, Basil had worn a rose in his buttonhole. How handsome he had looked in that bright blue suit, with that dark red rose! And he knew it, too. He couldn't help knowing it. First he stroked his hair, then his moustache; his teeth gleamed when he smiled.

"The headmaster's wife keeps on asking me to dinner. It's a perfect nuisance. I never get an evening to myself in that place."

"But can't you refuse?"

"Oh, well, it doesn't do for a man in my position to be unpopular."

Music's Gay Measure, wailed the voices. The willow trees, outside the high, narrow windows, waved in the wind. They had lost half their leaves. The tiny ones that clung wriggled like fishes caught on a line. "... I am not a marrying man. ..." The voices were silent; the piano waited.

"Quite good," said Miss Meadows, but still in such a strange, stony tone that the younger girls began to feel positively frightened. "But now that we know it, we shall take it with expression. As much expression as you can put into it. Think of the words, girls. Use your imaginations. *Fast! Ah, too Fast,*" cried Miss Meadows. "That ought to break out—a loud, strong *forte*—a lament. And then in the second line, *Winter Drear*, make that *Drear* sound as if a cold wind were blowing through it. *Dre-ear!*" said she so awfully that Mary Beazley, on the music stool, wriggled her spine. "The third line should be one cresendo. *Fleetly! Ah, Fleetly Music's Gay Measure*. Breaking on the first word of the last line, *Passes*. And then on the word, *Away*, you must begin to die ... to fade ... until *The Listening Ear* is nothing more than a faint whisper.... You can slow down as much as you like almost on the last line. Now, please."

Again the two light taps; she lifted her arms again. *Fast! Ah, too Fast*. "... and the idea of settling down fills me with nothing but disgust—" Disgust was what he had written. That was as good as to say their engagement was definitely broken off. Broken off! Their engagement! People had been surprised enough that she had got engaged. The Science Mistress would not believe it at first. But nobody had been as surprised as she. She was thirty. Basil was twenty-five. It had been a miracle, simply a miracle, to hear him say, as they walked home from church that very dark night, "You know, somehow or other, I've got fond of you." And he had taken hold of the end of her ostrich feather boa. *Passes away from the Listening Ear*.

"Repeat! Repeat!" said Miss Meadows. "More expression, girls! Once more!"

Fast! Ah, too Fast. The older girls were crimson; some of the younger ones began to cry. Big spots of rain blew against the windows, and one could hear the willows whispering, "... not that I do not love you...."

"But, my darling, if you love me," thought Miss Meadows, "I don't mind how much it is. Love me as little as you like." But she knew he didn't love her. Not to have cared enough to scratch out that word "disgust," so that she couldn't read it! *Soon Autumn yields unto Winter Drear.* She would have to leave the school, too. She could never face the Science Mistress or the girls after it got known. She would have to disappear somewhere. *Passes away.* The voices began to die, to fade, to whisper . . . to vanish. . . .

Suddenly the door opened. A little girl in blue walked fussily up the aisle, hanging her head, biting her lips, and twisting the silver bangle on her red little wrist. She came up the steps and stood before Miss Meadows.

"Well, Monica, what is it?"

"Oh, if you please, Miss Meadows," said the little girl, gasping, "Miss Wyatt wants to see you in the mistress's room."

"Very well," said Miss Meadows. And she called to the girls, "I shall put you on your honour to talk quietly while I am away." But they were too subdued to do anything else. Most of them were blowing their noses.

The corridors were silent and cold; they echoed to Miss Meadows' steps. The head mistress sat at her desk. For a moment she did not look up. She was as usual disentangling her eye-glasses, which had got caught in her lace tie. "Sit down, Miss Meadows," she said very kindly. And then she picked up a pink envelope from the blotting-pad. "I sent for you just now because this telegram has come for you."

"A telegram for me, Miss Wyatt?"

Basil! He had committed suicide, decided Miss Meadows. Her hand flew out, but Miss Wyatt held the telegram back a moment. "I hope it's not bad news," she said, so more than kindly. And Miss Meadows tore it open.

* * * *

"Pay no attention to letter, must have been mad, bought hat-stand to-day—Basil," she read. She couldn't take her eyes off the telegram.

"I do hope it's nothing very serious," said Miss Wyatt, leaning forward.

"Oh, no, thank you, Miss Wyatt," blushed Miss Meadows. "It's nothing bad at all. It's"—and she gave an apologetic little laugh—"it's from my *fiancé* saying that . . . saying that —" There was a pause. "I *see*," said Miss Wyatt. And another pause. Then—"You've fifteen minutes more of your class, Miss Meadows, haven't you?"

"Yes, Miss Wyatt." She got up. She half ran towards the door.

"Oh, just one minute, Miss Meadows," said Miss Wyatt. "I must say I don't approve of my teachers having telegrams sent to them in school hours, unless in case of very bad news, such as death," explained Miss Wyatt, "or a very serious accident, or something to that effect. Good news, Miss Meadows, will always keep, you know."

On the wings of hope, of love, of joy, Miss Meadows sped back to the music hall, up the aisle, up the steps, over to the piano.

"Page thirty-two, Mary," she said, "page thirty-two," and, picking up the yellow chrysanthemum, she held it to her lips to hide her smile. Then she turned to the girls, rapped with her baton: "Page thirty-two, girls. Page thirty-two."

> *We come here To-day with Flowers o'erladen,*
> *With Baskets of Fruit and Ribbons to boot,*
> *To-oo Congratulate. . . .*

"Stop! Stop!" cried Miss Meadows. "This is awful. This

is dreadful." And she beamed at her girls. "What's the matter with you all? Think, girls, think of what you're singing. Use your imagination. *With Flowers o'erladen. Baskets of Fruit and Ribbons to boot.* And *Congratulate.*" Miss Meadows broke off. "Don't look so doleful, girls. It ought to sound warm, joyful, eager. *Congratulate.* Once more. Quickly. All together. Now then!"

And this time Miss Meadows' voice sounded over all the other voices—full, deep, glowing with expression.

ECHO FROM ITHACA

* * * * * * * * *

* * * * *

by G. B. Stern

The well-known explorer had married beneath her.
Luckily for explorers under these circumstances, they are
often away from home. Every two or three years Clementina
Knox returned, tanned and triumphant, from something that
was vaguely known as "The Interior," always to find the
little house in South Kensington bright and steadfast as
ever, the hearth swept, the Irish wolf-hound, Cormac, bay-
ing ecstatically, and her patient mate—Penelope to a
modern Ulysses—waiting for her with a smile of rather
anxious welcome. The anxiety was because Arthur Reginald Knox knew that sooner or later, after Clementina had
shown him her latest trophies, and had decided where these
were to be put in the room she called her "den," and after
he in his turn, with a deprecating: "Oh, my dear, but that
will wait till to-morrow, you're tired, you can't possibly be
interested!" had shown her his own achievements in water-
colour, in photography, in weaving—after all that, he knew
well that she would turn to him with her shrewd tolerant
look, and ask him what fresh . . . suitors he had collected,
during her absence? Arthur Reginald, his mother would
have assured you proudly, had been popular-with-the-ladies
ever since he was quite a wee mite. He had always been
radiantly good-looking; and now, at the age of forty-two,
with his picturesque red-gold hair, his pointed, arrogant
beard of the same tint, his curling eyelashes, he was more
attractive than ever. Behind the beard and the hair and the

eyelashes, he was a simple, affectionate, gregarious soul. . . .
And what can be expected when a lonely photographer, with
sea-blue eyes, confesses to the most charming of his clientèle
that his wife is in "The Interior" again? A flutter of excitement: "Oh, but I've heard of her, of course . . . Clementina
Knox? . . . Oh, but she's famous! Is that really your wife?
Dear Florizel—" Florizel was his professional name "—
how proud you must be of her! And don't you ever *long* to
go with her? No, no, I see you can't leave your work. And
how do *you* pass the time while she's on her romantic
travels? So intrepid of her, I think. The Andes, too! Why,
she might meet some of those terrible Anzacs at any moment—Aztecs, I mean!"

"How do *you* pass the time?" . . . And so, of course, he
would offer to show the lovely lady his weaving. It was a
quaint, unusual hobby, and he did it very beautifully; his
ebony hand-loom, too, especially made for him, a present
from his wife, invariably raised little cries and screams of
delight and interest.

But directly Clementina returned, she scattered Arthur's
consolers so effectively that they never returned. And next
time she went away, he had to build up his little world from
the beginning. Her tolerance was for him, never for them.
But there were always fresh clients, fresh springs of sympathy, fresh excitement over his old-world hobby. All the
same, on this last occasion of Clementina's return, Arthur
Reginald had discovered in himself a gradual swell of exasperation at her offhand ways; exasperation at the lack
of consideration with which she treated his friends, his
pretty little friends; exasperation at the callous good-bye
which he knew would be in store for him in a few months,
directly she grew restless again.

Above all, exasperation whenever he entered her den.

He hated that den. It was so unwomanly and enormous . . . great stuffed beasts; fearful reminders of warfare from all periods and countries; skins and tusks and saddles; a rough-hewn block of stone with Inca markings, from Potosi; and now, worst of the lot, these two statues, gigantic, blank of face, brought from the South Sea island of her recent important discovery; smaller than Easter Island, but likewise containing the same type of stone figures remaining from some ancient tribal worship. They had attracted a crowd of pressmen, wanting to write them up, and to write *her* up, where she sat at her big, workman-looking desk, cigarette ash all over the place. . . . Not a womanly room! lacking even a canary singing in its cage!

He noted jealously that the hound Cormac seemed to prefer lying in there.

It is not all fun to be an explorer's husband. And quite suddenly they quarrelled. They had never quarrelled before. It was when Clementina announced at tea-time, over the crumpets, that she would be off again that day week, and that she had been busy collecting her equipment. Something Polar this time, he gathered from her casual explanations. And then Arthur Reginald, who had had rather a nervy day in the studio, photographing an octogenarian, two children, and a white-whiskered colonel—not at all one of his usual days!—Arthur Reginald cried disconsolately: "Off again? Can't you stop at home and settle down? Settle down like any other—" He stopped, and choked . . . took a mouthful of tea. . . .

Clementina scrutinised him with that quizzical half-smile of hers, not far removed from tenderness, but a hundred thousand miles removed from any more respectful emotion.

"Settle down?" she repeated. "Me? Settle down here, in this house? Why, what should I do?"

"You could write your experiences," stiffly from Arthur. He had been hurt by her inflection of "in this house." Surely he had made a very happy little home for her? He recalled, wistfully, the indiscriminate enthusiasm of Lady Pleasance Mortimer, of Miss Daphne Peacock, and young Mrs. Frank Wellsham, when he had first shown them over "The Restynge-Place." Even the name of the house had been invented by him as a subtle compliment to Clementina. Restynge-Place. . . . Well, why the devil couldn't she rest? Lady Pleasance Mortimer, Mrs. Wellsham, and Miss Daphne Peacock would so gladly have rested there . . . in his arms.

Arthur Reginald glared at his wife, as he repeated: "You could write your experiences."

"Not I!" laughed the explorer. "Too tame! I'd rather go out and rope in some more!"

"You never think of me, do you?"

She slightly raised her brows. "Like to come along?"

Florizel-Arthur would have hated to come along, and well she knew it. The question was merely another insult.

"You don't know when you're well off!" said Arthur, his repartee sinking to the class from which she had raised him.

Clementina decided to change the subject. They were having tea in the den, and she made some kindly remark about the handsome curtains which were being woven by him to hang across her tall windows, but which were not yet finished. It occurred to Arthur, in his smarting and foolhardy state of mind, that he might try and rouse her jealousy:

"I did finish the curtains for your windows several times

while you were away," quoth he, lightly; "but I always gave them to somebody else; somebody who *appreciated* them."

She remained unmoved, even on the subject of "somebody." . . . "By the way, Arthur, I do wish I could come back, for once, and not find you surrounded by a collection of yearning, goggling half-wits with eyes like Pekinese. It lets me down!"

Her husband banged his cup onto the table, and banged out of the house.

. . . He never knew quite how it happened, but presently he found himself rapidly striding round and round the Albert Memorial. In his frenzy, he must have rushed into Kensington Gardens, not noticing that he was being carried along by rage, as usually by intention, to what was secretly his favourite sanctuary; secretly, for he was a little ashamed of his preference. It was one thing to be mediaeval in his tastes —weaving, and all that!—but quite another to be just old-fashioned. Yet as a small boy, he had been fascinated by the Memorial. It was gold, all gold! and there were so many figures on it. You never came to the end of discovery, if you were a true Memorialite. And even since he was grown-up, in defiance of those who scoffed, Arthur Reginald found a curious sense of peace and rhythm descended upon him, strolling from Asia to Europe, from Europe to America, and from America to Africa, and so round again to the group called Asia. He always had a friendly nod for Asia's elephant, who held up, as to a palmist, an immense foot, the line of love crossed by fate, and dropping a little towards the Mount of Venus. . . . He sympathised with the sick-cow expression on the face of Europa's bull; and the camel was nice, too; and the sheep in the group which represented

Agriculture gave him a mellow harvest-and-sunset sort of feeling which he never got from Clementina. And then if you sauntered slowly up to the top flight of steps, circling the base of the memorial, there were Shakespeare and Dante sitting diffidently on the ground at the feet of Homer— which always made Arthur a little indignant, because he thought that Shakespeare should be in the middle! not Dante, certainly, who was just a foreigner, but Shakespeare! ... There were too many foreigners altogether, in the frieze of celebrities, and one day he meant to write to the papers about it. And at this loyal stage of meditation, Arthur Reginald usually lit another cigarette, and watched benevolently the passings and repassings of sight-seers less at home than himself at the Memorial: provincials and Americans. And he thought proudly of the British Empire, and wistfully of Clementina, far away in a less symbolised and more dangerous form of Asia, Africa, America....

But this evening, his mood was neither benevolent nor wistful. He had never before been aware that such tumult of rage existed within him. His heart felt like a clenched fist; his soul was like the wild sunset sinking to the west of Kensington Gardens, behind the dark bulk of the Prince Consort's statue. He even shook his fist at Raphael. His self-respect was in conflagration. ... It was all so unjust, so unjust! ... Why couldn't his wife be like other men's wives? Why couldn't his home be like other men's homes? Why had he been so patient, so long-suffering? And when his loneliness had groped for a little help, a little cosiness, a little company in the aching void, even then she had grudged him such harmless consolation ... "goggling half-wits with eyes like Pekinese!" ... Yes, she had come home, time after time, striding determined, a conqueror laden with pillage, and had shattered the little warm makeshift world that he had built up for himself. She could not even leave him that!

These ruthless modern Amazon women. . . .

Round and round and round the Albert Memorial. . . . Asia, Europe, America, Africa. . . . Africa, America, Europe, Asia. . . . *Exploring?* Bah! What good did exploring ever do anybody? And she had mocked at him and his hand-woven curtains and his clients, his pretty, pretty clients. . . . "Florizel has a positive genius for the profile!" . . . Arthur thought of his studio, he thought of the many profiles he had posed, delicately lifting the chin with his finger-tips, against a background of dusky clematis velvet. Clementina Knox alone had never sat for him. She had said, abruptly, that if she had to make a show of herself for publicity purposes, she would rather it were to a stranger. . . .

"I'm off next week!" Just that! Without pity or consideration . . . and that was married life! And in seven or eight months she might perhaps return with another beastly trophy to shove into her beastly den. . . . Ugly, hideous room! Arthur Reginald had always loathed it; now he wanted to destroy it, for it symbolised the whole difference between his wife, and the soft, sweet-hearted feminine, and, if the truth be indeed known, half-witted little wife of his dreams. Goaded by the contrast, anger swung into delirium. . . . "I *shan't* let her go! That's it!—I shan't *let* her go! I'll say 'no' next time she asks me! (But will she ask me?) I'll say 'no,' quite firmly!" muttered Clementina's husband, staring hard at the statue humped between himself and the sunset. The Prince Consort, presiding genius of the place which Arthur loved best. He felt a queer spasm of intimacy . . . a link. . . .

And then an inspiration: *"Assert yourself!"*

Yes, he would assert himself, powerfully. But why had he thought of that just now? Of course, yes . . . that famous incident told and re-told in every book he had ever read, of the Queen and her husband:

They had quarrelled, and the Prince Consort had locked the door of his room. Came an imperious tap.

"Who is it?"

"The Queen!" And he would not open.

For the second time: "Who is it?"

"The Queen!"

And yet again, for the third time: "Who is it?"

"Your wife, Albert."

And they lived happy ever after. . . .

That, then, was the right way to behave with an imperious, imperial woman. What should he, Arthur Knox, do, to show Clementina that in future she was to be no more than his wife, his loving, acquiescent little home-bird?

What should he do?

A picture which came he knew not whence, snapped into his mind. It showed him standing in her den, erect, inflexible, stern and yet gentle. The room around him was a ruin. Every one of her possessions were smashed to pulp, ground to powder. . . . He had wrecked it, deliberately, for it stood for all he hated most in her life. . . . "Who has done this?" . . . "Your husband, Clementina!" . . . A swift melting into his forgiving arms. He had expressed his will once and for all; no need ever to do it again.

Dare he? Had he the courage? Was it a good thing to do?

. . . The sun was almost down now. Arthur Knox stared at the Prince, solitary under his Gothic canopy. Half unconsciously, he besought encouragement; a signal, if it were possible. . . .

And then, quite clearly, he saw the statue move its hand.

One of the casual sight-seers at the Memorial had also
noticed the pigeon poised in sharp black relief against
sunset gold, on the Prince Consort's left knee. He enquired
of the little bearded man who sold postcards in the enclosure between the rail and the frieze: "Excuse me . . . Are
those birds—er—allowed up there?"

The postcard-vendor glanced scornfully at his silly inter-
locutor: "Well, they don't never ask, not that I knows of!"

. . . Another pigeon wheeled round Albert's bronze head,
and then slid down an invisible rush of wind to his mate.
A few seconds later, and the two birds, stirred by the same
impulse, soared away together till they were tiny curves
far above the roof of the Albert Hall.

Feeling like Zeus armed with thunderbolts of wrath,
Arthur Reginald crashed into the den of Clementina Knox,
traveller and explorer; and picking up the nearest of those
detestable trophies, which happened to be a slab of orbicu-
lar granite from Michigan, he hurled it furiously against the
head of a Nyasaland buffalo grinning at him from the
wall. . . . That would show them what sort of a man he was!

. . . Neither the granite nor the buffalo were in the least
affected by their unlooked-for contact. The granite dropped
with a thud to the floor . . . and Arthur, by impetus of his
own violence, stumbled over the head of a Kamchatkin
Brown Bear-skin lying across the threshold, and fell almost
as heavily. He picked himself up, hating the den more than
ever. . . . The den, symbol of courage and daring and hardi-
hood which he so woefully lacked. Never mind! His turn
now!

Unfortunately for him, the dauntless Mrs. Knox had been
all her life possessed by a quality of megalomania; perhaps

because she was so small and slim and wiry herself; nerves like the finest steel springs; delicate small shapes of hands and feet, ridiculous, considering what they had accomplished. Therefore she had a passion for all that was immense and tough. Her den had been built on to the garden space of the house. It was a huge room, and far from cosy. Even the great stone idols, did not look unnaturally tall in it. Her husband particularly disliked these stone idols. There had been so much talk about them; interviewers had appeared, striving to find out if there were a lighter and more popular side to the archaeological interest they had aroused; and learned professors had quarrelled on such points as whether, being smaller than the idols on Easter Island, they had been made several thousand years later by a race become degenerate? or several thousand years earlier, before the race was so powerful and had so many slave captives? Arthur Reginald glared with bloodshot eyes at the Whitsun Island idols. With a certain rigid imperturbable courtesy, they stared back. Then, exasperated beyond all reason, he hurled himself upon one of them. The idol merely looked as though a fly had walked across its chest. . . . Arthur, bruised and baffled, sought for something more effective with which to attack. The walls were a gleaming pattern of weapons of every sinister shape; needless to say, they were all big and terribly heavy.

Presently might have been seen the spectacle of Arthur Reginald lunging at a South Sea idol about eight feet high, with an assegai. . . . "Qu'il est drôle, ce petit bonhomme là!" remarked the idol—or words to that effect—to his brother idol. Arthur threw down the assegai. He was already sweating from his endeavours, but the den looked much the same as when he had entered it. He rolled his eyes round in search of further missiles; there were all sorts of lumps and rocks and crags lying about; he seized a pumiceous bomb, and threw it at the idol. It hit the stuffed Persian tiger, and rebounded. In his ordinary moments, Arthur would hardly have been capable of lifting the great chunk of smoky quartz from China, or the volcanic tear, or the block of stilbite which now, disregarding direction, and in his mood of abnormal fury, he threw again and again against the impassivity of the guardians of the doorway.... This room, this damnable room! ... He was able to break nothing but his own heart. At the end of what seemed like hours of smashing destruction, he had created a preposterous confusion, and had snapped the tip off one horn of an East African white oryx. No more than that. Staggering over a heap of skins, tusks, and leather ox-saddles, he hammered desperately with a pair of rhinoceros tusks at the bristly whiskers of an incredibly patronising sea-elephant from the Crozet Islands. But his spirit was flagging ... exhausted. It had first begun to recoil when he had tried to seize a vast specimen of meteoric iron, so that he could batter the huge smooth shell of a land-tortoise who might just as well have stopped in the Siwalik Hills, for all the impression that England and Arthur Reginald could succeed in scratching upon him. ...

Arthur's breath was coming in great sobs ... his hair was wild and disarranged, streaking his forehead ... his knuckles were bleeding in a hopeless sort of way.

It was upon this tableau that Clementina Knox made her entrance.

"Why—who's made all this mess?" she asked, amazed.

Arthur Reginald dropped the tusks, and swung round blindly towards the door. Here was his chance; now he should have delivered the speech in which he had planned to assert himself for ever as the strong dominant male: "Your husband, Clementina . . ."

. . . Not an hour ago, at the Albert Memorial, he had pleaded for a signal. Had the signal betrayed him?

He put up his hand, as though to brush away a blur of objects that swam dizzily in front of his sight: huge, tough, vindictive heads of beasts, iron and stone and horn and leather, things that would not shatter, would not crack even, for all his maddened efforts to show himself conqueror of the small, slim creature who had collected them. . . .

She repeated: "What *are* you doing, Arthur?"

And he replied: "My dear, I was just—well, I—I was just rearranging your den, for a surprise. It . . . looks a bit untidy, I'm afraid, but I'll soon tidy it up!"

A GOURDFUL OF GLORY

* * * * * * * * *

* * * * *

by Margaret Laurence

You could walk through the entire market and look at every stall, but never would you see calabashes and earthen pots any better than those sold by Mammii Ama. She was honest—true as God, she really was. You might claim that there were as many honest traders here as there were elephants, and Mammii Ama would understand your meaning, and laugh, and agree with you. But she would let you know she was the one old cow-elephant that never yet died off.

She was a petty trader. A few market women grew rich and became queen mammies, but Mammii Ama was not one of these. She got by. She lived. Nobody ever got the better of her, but she wasn't one to cheat her customers. She handled good stock. She wasn't like some of those shifty mammies who bought cheap and sold at the regular price the gourd with the faint seam of a crack right in the bottom where you wouldn't notice it until the soup began to leak out. She never sold flawed pots and bowls, either, a bit damaged in the firing so that they broke if you laughed in the same room with them. Such a trick was not Mammii Ama's way. The odd cull, maybe, she would admit. A few could always slip into a lot. You know how it is. A trader woman has to live, after all.

The cockerels, piercing the dawn grey with shrill and scarlet voices, awoke no earlier than Mammii Ama. Expertly, she bunched her fish-patterned cloth around her, bound on a headscarf of green and glossy artificial silk, and was ready for the day. She puffed the charcoal embers into flame, plonked on the tin kettle, brewed tea and ate some cold boiled yam.

Comfort was still lying curled up on the straw mat. One always hated to waken a sleeping child. Mammii Ama gently shook her granddaughter, and Comfort sat up, dazed, like a parrot with all its feather ruffled. She was soon dressed; not yet five years old, she wore only a shame-cloth, a mere flutter of beaded red rag around her middle and between her legs.

Then they were off. Wait—a last thought. Did Adua sleep peacefully? Was she covered? If you sweated, sleeping, you got a chill in your belly and you had pain passing water for evermore. Quiet as a watch-night, Mammii Ama padded across the hut to the iron cot where her snoring daughter lay. Adua was properly covered—the blanket was drawn up to her neck, and all you could see of her was her head with its wiry hair that she was always straightening with hot pull-irons, and her face, breathing softly and brown under its matting of white powder from the night before. Mammii Ama did not understand why her daughter daubed herself with talcum until she looked like a fetish priestess in a funeral parade. Many things about Adua were difficult to comprehend. The high-heel shoes, for instance, which hurt and were all but impossible to walk on. Teeter this way, lurch that—a fine business. The woman's anklebones would snap one of these days—but try to tell her. And the palaver about the name—a lunacy. Adua called herself Marcella, and insisted that everyone else do the same. It was not like the granddaughter's name. Comfort—a decent name. A mission name, true, but it had lived here a long time, until it seemed to have been African always. But Marcella—who ever heard of such a name? Mammii Ama couldn't bring herself to speak it. She called her daughter "moon woman" or "choice of kings," and Adua, who was—you had to admit it—very vain, liked to hear those names as she preened herself.

Still, she was a good daughter. She brought home money— worked all night for it. A club girl, she was, at the Weekend in Wyoming, and Mammii Ama loved her more dearly than life, and felt for her a shy and surprised pride, for the daughter was certainly a beauty, not a cow-elephant like her mother.

Mammii Ama looked once more on the powdered and sleeping face, then she was gone, shutting quietly behind her the packing-case door of the mud-brick shanty.

Mammii Ama took the child's hand while they clambered onto the crowded bus. She paid her fare, and the bus, with a rumble like the belly of a giant, jolted off down the road and into the city.

The market was already filling with sellers. The best hunter got an early start, Mammii Ama would say. You'd never catch a fat cutting-grass by sleeping late. As she spread out her wares in front of her stall, Mammii Ama sang. She sang in pidgin, so that every passer-by, whatever his language, would understand.

> *"Mammii Ama sell all fine pot,*
> *Oh oh Mammii Ama!*
> *She no t'ief you, she no make palavah,*
> *Oh oh Mammii Ama—"*

And the girl child, squatting in dust as she arranged just so the stacks of brown earthen bowls, the big-bellied black cooking-pots, added to the refrain her high and not quite true-pitched voice.

"Oh oh Mammii Ama—"

Everywhere there were voices, and sweet singing bodies. Everywhere the market women's laughter, coarse and warm as the touch of a tongue. It was still early, and the morning cooks had not yet arrived to buy vegetables and meat for the Europeans.

Moki was already perched atop his firewood. He wiped the rheum from his eyes with an end of his dirty turban. He was old, and his eyes ran mucus, especially in the morning. He was not a Moslem, but his nephew, who died of a worm in the guts, had been one, so Moki always wore a turban in memory of him. No one knew where Moki came from. He didn't know himself. He knew the name of his village, but not the country where it was, and he knew the names of his people's gods. He had come here who knows how long ago, with a Hausa caravan, and had somehow lost the trader who hired him to carry headload. Now he sold pieces of firewood, which he gathered each evening in the bush.

"Morny, Mistah Moki! I greet you!" Mammii Ama called, and the old man fake-bowed to her as though she were a queen mother.

On the other side, a Hausa man was hanging up his white-and-black wool mats and huge pointed hats and long embroidered robes which only men tall as the Hausas could wear. Sabina the cloth-seller snapped at a small boy who pissed beside her stall, complaining that he was spraying her second-best bolts, draped outside to catch the eye. The small boy's mother threw a coconut husk which caught him on the ear, and he ran off, leaking and howling.

T'reepenny, who looked more ancient than the gods,

creaked and trembled up to Mammii Ama's stall. Her hands, bony as tree roots and frail as grass, lugged along the bucket of gourd spoons, half of them broken. She had no stall. She had no money to rent one, so Mammii Ama allowed her to sit beside the calabash-and-pot stall with her bucket. She only said one word, ever. Maybe she only knew one. "T'ree-penny," she would quiver and quaver. "T'reepenny, t'ree-penny," over and over like a brainfever bird, as she held up the gourd spoons for all to admire. She was pleased if she got one penny. Only from white women, rich and gullible, had she ever received as much as three.

With the wares arranged, Mammii Ama was light in heart. Now she began to recall last night's rally. She had gone with the others in the Association of Market Women. They all wore new cloth, in the party's colours, red and white and green. What a thing it had been! Her well-fleshed hips remembered their jigglings and marvellous convolutions in the parade. Her shoulders and hearty arms remembered the touch of others' arms and shoulders as the market women marched. Four abreast, they entered the meeting-place like a charging army, like an army with spears of fire, with rifles fashioned of power and glory. And they all shouted together —loud as a thousand lorry horns, loud as the sea—"Free-Dom!"

And he had been there, the lovely boy they loved so well, the Show-Boy. He spoke to them of the day that was coming, the day of freedom. And they shouted with one voice, and they cheered with one voice. They were his women, his mothers and his brides.

"Hey, you, Sabina!" Mammii Ama shouted. "Were you at the rally?"

"Naturally," the shriek came back. "Didn't you see me, Mammii Ama? I was at the back, in between Mercy Mensah and that old Togo woman, whatever her name is."

"I was at the front," Mammii Ama said loudly, but with modesty.

"I was there, too," Moki chipped in.

Everyone laughed.

"Wha-at? I never knew you were a market woman, Moki," Mammii Ama bellowed.

"When you get to my age, it's all the same," Moki replied evenly. "Man—woman—what does it matter? We all eat. We all die."

An outburst of chitter-chatter. "Don't tell me that story, Moki!" "Maybe it's an old muzzle-loader, but I'll bet it still fires!" And so on.

"What did you think of it, Sabina, the rally?" Mammii Ama continued, when the gust of ribaldry faded.

Sabina shrugged. She was thin, and her mouth always turned down, as though she had just swallowed a piece of rotten fish.

"Well, it's a lot of talk, if you ask me," she said. "Free-Dom. Independence. All right—the white men go. So, then? We'll still be haggling over tuppence at our stalls, my friends."

Mammii Ama jumped to her feet and shook her head and both fists at Sabina.

"Ei! Somebody here is like a crocodile? Yes, somebody acts like the crocodile who crawls in the mud of the river. He lives in the river mud—and he thinks the whole world is only river mud. Oh, blind! Blind!"

She appealed to the others.

"Free-Dom—it's like the sun," she cried. "You have to crawl out of the river mud or you can't see it."

Moki muttered and went on cleaning his eyes. Old T'ree-penny nodded her head. She agreed in this way with everything Mammii Ama said. She didn't understand, but she agreed. Whatever Mammii Ama said must be right. The Hausa man stared—he spoke no Ga.

Sabina went on shrugging, and Mammii Ama grew so furious she rushed over to Sabina's stall and burst into fresh argument. She grew inspired. She no longer cared about Sabina. Around her, the market women gathered. They cried "Ha—ei!" when she paused for breath. They swayed and chanted to the rhythm of Mammii Ama.

"Go call all de market woman!" Mammii Ama cried, this time in pidgin, to captivate a wider audience. "Tell dem say 'Free-Dom'! Go call all de market woman—say, you no go sell befoah five minute. You sell Free-Dom dis time. What dis t'ing, what dis Free-Dom? He be strong, he be fine too much. Ju-ju man he no got such t'ing, such power word. Dis Free-Dom he be sun t'ing, same sun he be shine. Hey, you market woman, you say 'Money sweet—I be poor woman, nothing with, on'y one penny. I no 'gree dis Free-Dom, I no be fit for chop him.' Oh—oh—I t'ink you be bushwoman, no got sense. I no 'gree for you. I tell you, dis Free-Dom he be sweet sweet t'ing. You wait small, you see I tell you true. Market woman all dey be queen mammy den."

Moki stopped his eye-wiping and waved a piece of firewood, roaring encouragement to his friend Mammii Ama. The Hausa man uttered sombre cries in his own tongue—"Allah knows it! Has not the Prophet himself said the same? It will be shown at the Last Day!" T'reepenny, carried away by excitement, grasped a gourd spoon in either hand and executed a sort of dance, back bent and stiff-kneed, all by herself, until her unsteady breath gave out and she sank down beside her bucket once more, chirping her mournful word.

Sabina, feeling herself outnumbered, began to weep, beg-

ging them all not to forget her unfortunate past. If she
seemed sour, she sobbed, they knew why.

Mammii Ama immediately grew sympathetic. She broke
off and put an arm around Sabina's shoulder. A terrible
thing it must have been, she agreed. Enough to mark a
person for life.

Sabina had once had a wealthy lover—well, not wealthy,
perhaps, but certainly nicely fixed. A clerk, he was, a man
in a government office. He always seemed healthy, Sabina
used to say. He seemed so strong, so full of life, so full of
love. How that man would do it! Again and again—why,
half a dozen times in a single night, that was nothing to
him, Sabina said, simply nothing.

Then one night, his heart swelled and burst, and he died,
just like that. He was with Sabina at the time. They had
gone to sleep, still together. At least, she had gone to sleep.
A little later, feeling cramped and trying to turn, she had
wakened to find a dead man there. Dead as a gutted fish,
and his eyes wide open. Sabina got a baby that night, it
turned out, and she went around saying her child had been
given her by a dead man. She was sure of it. She screeched
and cried. A child begotten by a corpse—who could stand
the thought? No one was surprised when the baby was born
dead.

The women clucked softly. Mammii Ama, ashamed of her
attack, soothed and soothed in her full mother-voice.

"There, my red lily. Cry, then. It is nothing. I am a fool;
I have a head like a calabash, empty."

Into the hush-hushing throng of women ran Comfort. Her
face was frightened and excited.

"Mammii Ama! Mammii Ama! A white woman has come
to your stall!"

And Mammii Ama looked amazed, dumbfounded, only

partly in mockery of the child. Hastily she hitched her cloth up around her, and flew back.

"Ei—what a madness!"

She went running along like a girl, like a young girl at her first outdooring. She carried her weight lightly, and her breasts bounced as she bounced over gutter and path, over smouldering charcoal burner, over the sleeping babies with blackflies at the edge of their nostrils.

"Who is the young virgin fleeing from her seducer?" Moki shouted as she approached. "Oh oh Mammii Ama!"

The white woman was thin and tall. She had very little flesh on her, just yellow hide over bones, and her eyes were such a pale blue they seemed not to be there at all—only the jelly of the eyeball, nothing to see with. She was holding a brown earthen bowl in her hands.

Mammii Ama regained her breath.

"Madam—I greet you," she said with hoarse cheerfulness.

The white woman smiled uncertainly and looked over her shoulder. Mammii Ama looked, too, and it was Ampadu standing there.

Ampadu was a clerk. He had a good job. One heard he had influence. He was a really educated man—he knew not only reading and writing but also the work of account books and typewriters. Mammii Ama, who could neither read nor write, and who kept her accounts in her head with never a mistake in twenty-four years, was greatly impressed with Ampadu's power over words and numbers. She did not tell him so—in fact, she constantly made fun of him. They were distantly related, and Ampadu, who understood her unexpressed pride in this relationship, took her jibes in an easy-natured way.

She clapped him on the shoulder. He was neatly dressed

in a white shirt and grey flannel trousers. How prosperous he looked. And his rimmed spectacles, how well they suited him.

"Ampadu! I greet you!" she cried in Ga. "How are you, great government man? Do they still say your pen is more active than your love-branch? Hey—you, Moki! Did you know this? When the old chief's young wife wanted a lover, she sent for Ampadu's pen!"

The clerk laughed, but not wholeheartedly. He patted his stomach in embarrassment. Mammii Ama, realizing Ampadu was accompanying the white woman, began to roll her eyes and pretended to stagger.

"What's this, Ampadu? What's this? What's all this about?"

Ampadu held up his hand, like a policeman stopping a lorry.

"She wants to see the market," he hissed. "She's the wife of my new boss. Mammii Ama, please be sensible, I implore you. She wants to buy a calabash, God knows why."

The white woman was growing impatient.

"Ampadu—ask her what she'll take for this bowl, please."

"Ten shillings," Mammii Ama replied without hesitation.

"Ten shillings!" the white woman cried, and even Ampuda looked stunned.

Mammii Ama seized the bowl from her hands.

"See, madam—dis one, he be fine too much. No be bad one. Look—put your fingah heah—you feel? All fine—nevah broke, dis one. Ten shilling, madam."

"How much is the usual price?" the white woman asked Ampadu.

Ampadu scuffed his shoes in the dust. Mammii Ama felt quite sorry for him, but she had to try hard not to laugh.

"Usual price?" Ampadu appeared to search his memory.

"Let me see, what is the usual price? I am sorry madam— I am afraid I don't really know. My wife, you see, buys all the cooking-pots—"

"Ten shilling!" shouted Mammii Ama in a huge voice. "All time, meka price he be ten shilling! I tell you true, madam, I no t'ief you."

"Five shillings," the white woman offered.

"Nine shilling sixpence—for you."

They settled at length on six shillings, to Mammii Ama's well-disguised delight. The white woman then bought a black cooking-pot and two calabashes. Mammii Ama was amazed. What could such a woman want with cooking-pots and calabashes? Were Europeans living like poor Africans all of a sudden? Mammii Ama felt excited and confused. The order of things was turning upside down, but pleasurably, in a way that provided food for speculation and gossip.

When the white woman was gone, they all discussed it. Who could understand such a thing? Mammii Ama, dusting and rearranging her stock of pots and bowls, began one of her speeches.

"Hey! Stranger woman, listen to me. Do you feed your man from a calabash you bought in the market? Does your man eat from a bowl made of river clay? Ei! The gourdvine dances—he shakes his leaves with laughter. Ei! The river fish drown in their laughter. Your own dishes—are they not white as a silver shilling? They are white as the egret's feathers, when he sleeps in the baobab tree. If the fine vessels displease you, give them to my granddaughter. Yes! Give them to Comfort, the lovely and dear one—"

Mammii Ama turned the last bit into a song, and sang it all day. Some of the others joined in the refrain, varying it from time to time for amusement.

> *"Yes! Give them to the woodseller,*
> *Give them to Moki, the lovely one—"*

Mammii Ama added a stanza in pidgin, so everyone around would know she was no longer cross at Sabina.

> *"Meka you dash dem for Sabina,*
> *She fine too much, same been-to gal,*
> *She like all fine t'ing—"*

A week later, the white woman returned, this time alone. Mammii Ama greeted her like an old friend. The white woman bought a gourd spoon from T'reepenny, and haggled with Mammii Ama over the price of another bowl. Finally, Mammii Ama could restrain her curiosity no longer.

"Madam—why you buy African pot?"

The white woman smiled.

"I want to use them for ashtrays."

"Ashtray! For dem cig'rette?" Mammii Ama could not believe her ears. "You no got fine one, madam?"

"Oh—I have lots of others," the woman said, "but I like these. They're so beautifully shaped."

Mammii Ama could not credit it.

"An dem calabash? Madam chop *fu-fu* now?"

"I use the shallow ones to put groundnuts in," the woman explained. "For small-chop with drinks. The big ones I'm using for plants."

"Free-Dom time, meka all African get dem fine dish," Mammii Ama mused. "I look-a dem na Kingsway store. Fine dish, shine too much."

She stopped herself. It would not do, for business, to admit she would like to use fine white dishes. She even felt a little guilty at the thought. Were not her calabashes and bowls the best in the market? But still—

The white woman was looking at her oddly.

"You don't mean to tell me that you think you'll all be given—what did you say?—shiny dishes, when Independence comes?"

Mammii Ama did not know whether she believed it or not. But she grew stubborn.

"I tell you true!" Speaking the words, she became immediately convinced of their absolute truth. "Market woman, all dey be same queen mammy den."

"Is that what freedom means to you?" the woman asked.

Mammii Ama felt somehow that she was being attacked at her very roots.

"What dis t'ing, what dis Free-Dom? You no savvy Free-Dom palavah, madam. He be strong, dis Free-Dom, he be power word."

"You're free now," the woman said. "We give you justice. I'll wager you won't have it then."

The woman did not speak pidgin. Mammii Ama could not follow every word, but she detected the meaning. The white woman was against Free-Dom. Mammii Ama was not surprised, of course. Nor was she angry. What else would you expect of Europeans? When she spoke, it was not to the white woman. It was to the market, to the city, to every village quiet in the heat of the sun.

She spread her arms wide, as though she would embrace the whole land. She felt the same as she had once long ago, when she went to meet her young man in the grove. She was all tenderness and longing; she was an opening moonflower, filled with the seeds of life everlasting.

"Dis Free-Dom he be sun t'ing," she cried. "Same sun, he be shine. I no 'gree for Eur'pean. I 'gree for Free-Dom."

The woman looked thoughtful.

"Your leader seems popular among the market women."

"Ha—aah! He fine too much. He savvy all t'ing. He no forget we. Market women all dey come queen mammy. All—all—"

She stuttered and stopped. The Free-Dom speech seemed to have lost something of its former grandeur. Now Mammii Ama's words would not rise to her heights. Earthbound, she grasped for the golden lightning with which to illumine the sky. She found it.

"Dat time, you t'ink we pay wen we deah go for bus?" she cried. "We no pay! At all! Nevah one penny."

The white woman still peered. Then she laughed, a dry sound, like Moki breaking firewood.

"You really think the buses will be free after Independence?"

"I hear so," Mammii Ama said, truthfully. Then, feeling her faith not stated with sufficient strength, "Be so! Meka come Free-Dom nevah one penny for we. We go for bus free, free, free!"

Her words had the desired effect. The white woman was staring at her, certainly, staring with wide eyes. But in her face was an expression Mammii Ama did not understand. Who was this stranger, and why did she come here with her strange laughter and strange words and a strange look on her skull-face? Why didn't she go away?

Mammii Ama frowned. Then she heaved her shoulders in a vast shrug and turned back to her stall.

"Hey, you, Comfort! Hasn't the village woman come yet with the new calabashes?"

Soon, with the white woman gone, everything was in order, everything was itself once more, known and familiar.

> "*Mammii Ama sell all fine pot,*
> *Oh oh Mammii Ama!*

* * * *

> *She no t'ief you, she no make palavah,*
> *Oh oh Mammii Ama!"*

The white woman did not come again for a long time,
and Mammii Ama forgot about her. Things weren't going
so well. Both Adua and the child got sick—skin burning all
over, belly distended. Mammii Ama went to a dealer in
charms. Then she went to a dealer in roots and herbs. She
spent, altogether, six pounds four shillings and ninepence.
But it did no good. Adua wouldn't drink the brew the herb-
dealer concocted, nor would she allow Mammii Ama to
give it to the child. When the fetish priest came to the
shanty, Adua lay with her head covered by the blanket, not
wanting to see him, but afraid to send him away. Then
Adua insisted that Mammii Ama take Comfort to the hospital to see the doctor. Mammii Ama was very much op-
posed to the idea, but one did not dare argue with a sick
person. She took the child. They waited three days before
they could see the doctor, and Mammii Ama was in a
panic, thinking of her empty market stall, and no money
coming in. She had a little money saved, but it was almost
gone now. Finally, the doctor gave Comfort a bottle of
medicine, and Mammii Ama, when they arrived home, gave
some of it to Adua as well. Slowly the sickness went away,
withdrawing a speck of its poison at a time. Adua went
back to work, but Comfort was still too weak to help in the
market.

That was always the way—sometimes you had luck;
you were well; the coins in the wooden box grew; you
bought a little meat, a little fish, a bowl of lamb's blood for
the stew. Then—bam! Fever came, or somebody robbed
you, or nobody needed pots and calabashes that month.
And you were back where you started, eating only *garri*

and lucky to have anything. You got by somehow. If you couldn't live, you died, and that was that.

But then a great thing happened. Not in the ordinary run of exciting things, like Moki killing a small python, or Sabina getting pregnant again, this time by a live man. No—nothing like that at all. This was a great thing, the greatest of all great things.

Independence.

The time came. Everyone was surprised when the time actually came, although they'd been expecting it for so long. It was like a gift—a piece of gold that somebody dashed you for nothing.

Mammii Ama was so excited she could hardly breathe. The night before the Day, everyone gathered at the Parliament building, everyone who could dance or walk or totter, even old T'reepenny, who nearly got broken like a twig by the crowd until Mammii Ama staunchly elbowed a path for her. And there at midnight the white man's flag came down, and the new flag went up—so bright, and the black star so strong and shining, the new flag of the new land. And the people cried with one voice: "Now—now we are Free!"

The Day—who could describe it? Commoners and princes, all together. The priest-kings of the Ga people, walking stately and slow. The red-and-gold umbrellas of the proud Akan chiefs, and their golden regalia carried aloft by the soul-bearers, sword-bearers, spokesmen, guards. From the northern desert, the hawk-faced chiefs in tent-like robes. The shouting young men, the girls in new cloth, the noise and the dancing, the highlife music, the soldiers in their scarlet jackets. The drums beating and beating for evermore. The feasting. The palm wine, everybody happy. Free-Dom.

Mammii Ama sang and shouted until her voice croaked like a tree toad's. She drank palm wine. She danced like a young girl. Everybody was young. Everybody's soul was just born this minute. A day to tell your grandchildren and their children. "Free-Dom shone, silver as stars—oh, golden as sun. The day was here. We saw it. We sang it and shouted."

The day, of course, like any other day, had to finish sometime. Mammii Ama, exhausted, found her way home through the still-echoing streets. Then she slept.

The next morning Mammii Ama did not rise quite so early. The tea and boiled yam tasted raw in her mouth. She swallowed her cold bile and marched out.

Only when the bus drew to a stop did she remember. She climbed on, cheerful now, full of proud expectancy. She was about to push her way through the standing people near the door, when the driver touched her arm.

"Hey—you! You no pay yet."

She looked at him shrewdly.

"Wey you say? You t'ief me? I no pay now."

"So? Why you no pay?"

Mammii Ama folded her arms and regarded him calmly. "Free-Dom time, meka not one penny for we. I hear it."

The driver sighed heavily.

"De t'ing wey you hear, he no be so," he said crossly. "Meka you pay you fare. Now—one-time!"

Some of the other passengers were laughing. Mammii Ama scarcely heard them. Her eyes were fixed on the driver. He was not deceiving her—she could read it in his tired, exasperated face.

Without a word, she took out the coin and dropped it in the metal fare-box.

That day the white woman visited the market again. Mammii Ama, piling bowls in neat stacks, looked up and saw her standing there. The white woman held up a calabash and asked how much.

"Twelve shilling," Mammii Ama said abruptly, certain that would be enough to send the woman away.

To her utter astonishment, however, the woman paid without a murmur. As Mammii Ama reached out and took the money, she realized that the calabash was only an excuse.

"How were your Independence celebrations?" the white woman smiled. "Did you have a good time?"

Mammi Ama nodded but she did not speak.

"Oh, by the way—" the white woman said in a soft voice. "How did you get on with the bus this morning?"

Mammi Ama stared mutely. She, the speech-maker, was bereft of speech. She was more helpless than T'reepenny. She did not have even one word. She could feel her body trembling. The fat on her arms danced by itself, but not in joy. The drummer in her heart was beating a frenzy. Her heart hurt so much she thought she would fall down there in the dust, while the yellow skull of the woman looked and tittered.

Then, mercifully, the word was revealed to her. She had her power once more. Her drumming heart told her what to do. Snake-swift, Mammii Ama snatched back the calabash, at the same time thrusting the coins into the woman's hand.

"You no go buy from Mammii Ama! You go somewhere. You no come heah. I no need for you money."

She felt a terrible pang as she realized what had happened. She had parted with twelve shillings. She must be

going mad. But she would not turn back now. She took
another belligerent step, and the yellow menacing skull
retreated a little more. She spoke clearly, slowly, emphasiz-
ing each word.

"I no pay bus dis time," she said. "Bus—he—be free!
You hear? Free!"

Inspired, Mammii Ama lifted the gourd vessel high
above her head, and it seemed to her that she held not a
brittle brown calabash but the world. She held the world
in her strong and comforting hands.

"Free-Dom he come," she cried, half in exultation, half
in longing. "Free-Dom be heah now, dis minute!"

The sun rolled like an eye in its giant socket. The lightning swords of fire danced in the sky.

She became calm. She knew what was what. She knew
some things would happen, and others—for no reason apparent to her—would not. And yet, there was a truth in
her words, more true than reality. Setting down the calabash, she readjusted her fish-patterned cloth above her
breasts. She looked disinterestedly at her former customer.
The white woman was only a woman—only a bony and
curious woman, not the threatening skull-shape at all.

She watched the white woman go, and then she turned
back to her stall. She picked up the calabash and set it with
the rest. An ordinary calabash, nothing in it. Where was
the glory she had so certainly known only a moment before? Spilled out now, evaporated, gone. The clank of the
coin in the fare-box echoed again in her head, drowning
the heart's drums. She felt weary and spent as she began
stacking the earthen pots once more. A poor lot—she would
be lucky to get ninepence apiece. They seemed heavy to
her now—her arms were weighted down with them. It
would continue so, every day while her life lasted. Soon she

would be an old woman. Was death a feast-day, that one should have nothing else to look forward to?

Then a voice, hoarse as a raven's, began to sing. It was Moki the woodseller, and as he sang he beat out the rhythm with one of his gnarled sticks. Nearby, others took up the song. Sabina, singing, wrapped her cover-cloth more tightly and swaggered a little in front of her stall so they could see her belly was beginning to swell with the new, good child. The Hausa man donned one of his gilt-beaded hats and waggled his head in mock solemnity. Ancient T'reepenny shuffled in her solitary dance.

Mammii Ama, looking from one to the other, understood their gift and laughed her old enduring laughter and sang with them.

> *"Mammii Ama sell all fine pot,*
> *Oh oh Mammii Ama—"*

She was herself again, known and familiar. And yet— there was something more, something that had not been before. She tried to think what it was, but it eluded her. She could feel it, though. So that the others might know, too, she added to her old chant a verse no one had ever heard her sing before.

> *"Mammii Ama, she no come rich.*
> *Ha—ei! Be so. On'y one penny.*
> *She nevah be shame, she no fear for nothing.*
> *D' time wey come now, like queen she shine."*

And they caught the rhythm, and the faith, and the new words. Mammii Ama straightened her plump shoulders. Like a royal palm she stood, rooted in magnificence, spreading her arms like fronds, to shelter the generations.

A GOLD SLIPPER

* * * * * * * * *

' * * * * *

by Willa Cather

Marshall McKann followed his wife and her friend Mrs. Post down the aisle and up the steps to the stage of the Carnegie Music Hall with an ill-concealed feeling of grievance. Heaven knew he never went to concerts, and to be mounted upon the stage in this fashion, as if he were a "highbrow" from Sewickley, or some unfortunate with a musical wife, was ludicrous. A man went to concerts when he was courting, while he was a junior partner. When he became a person of substance he stopped that sort of nonsense. His wife, too, was a sensible person, the daughter of an old Pittsburgh family as solid and well-rooted as the McKanns. She would never have bothered him about this concert had not the meddlesome Mrs. Post arrived to pay her a visit. Mrs. Post was an old school friend of Mrs. McKann, and because she lived in Cincinnati she was always keeping up with the world and talking about things in which no one else was interested, music among them. She was an aggressive lady, with weighty opinions, and a deep voice like a jovial bassoon. She had arrived only last night, and at dinner she brought it out that she could on no account miss Kitty Ayrshire's recital; it was, she said, the sort of thing no one could afford to miss.

When McKann went into town in the morning he found that every seat in the music-hall was sold. He telephoned his wife to that effect, and, thinking he had settled the matter, made his reservation on the 11:25 train for New York.

He was unable to get a drawing-room because this same
Kitty Ayrshire had taken the last one. He had not intended
going to New York until the following week, but he preferred to be absent during Mrs. Post's incumbency.

In the middle of the morning, when he was deep in his
correspondence, his wife called him up to say the enter-
prising Mrs. Post had telephoned some musical friends in
Sewickley and had found that two hundred folding-chairs
were to be placed on the stage of the concert-hall, behind
the piano, and that they would be on sale at noon. Would he
please get seats in the front row? McKann asked if they
would not excuse him, since he was going to New York on
the late train, would be tired, and would not have time to
dress, etc. No, not at all. It would be foolish for two women
to trail up to the stage unattended. Mrs. Post's husband always accompanied her to concerts, and she expected that
much attention from her host. He needn't dress, and he
could take a taxi from the concert-hall to the East Liberty
station.

The outcome of it all was that, though his bag was at
the station, here was McKann, in the worst possible humour, facing the large audience to which he was well known,
and sitting among a lot of music students and excitable old
maids. Only the desperately zealous or the morbidly curious
would endure two hours in those wooden chairs, and he sat
in the front row of this hectic body, somehow made a party
to a transaction for which he had the utmost contempt.

When McKann had been in Paris, Kitty Ayrshire was
singing at the Comique, and he wouldn't go to hear her
—even there, where one found so little that was better to
do. She was too much talked about, too much advertised;
always being thrust in an American's face as if she were

something to be proud of. Perfumes and petticoats and cutlets were named for her. Some one had pointed Kitty out to him one afternoon when she was driving in the Bois with a French composer—old enough, he judged, to be her father—who was said to be infatuated, carried away by her. McKann was told that this was one of the historic passions of old age. He had looked at her on that occasion, but she was so befrilled and befeathered that he caught nothing but a graceful outline and a small, dark head above a white ostrich boa. He had noted with disgust, however, the stooped shoulders and white imperial of the silk-hatted man beside her, and the senescent line of his back. McKann described to his wife this unpleasing picture only last night, while he was undressing, when he was making every possible effort to avert this concert party. But Bessie only looked superior and said she wished to hear Kitty Ayrshire sing, and that her "private life" was something in which she had no interest.

Well, here he was; hot and uncomfortable, in a chair much too small for him, with a row of blinding footlights glaring in his eyes. Suddenly the door at his right elbow opened. Their seats were at one end of the front row; he had thought they would be less conspicuous there than in the centre, and he had not forseen that the singer would walk over him every time she came upon the stage. Her velvet train brushed against his trousers as she passed him. The applause which greeted her was neither overwhelming nor prolonged. Her conservative audience did not know exactly how to accept her toilette. They were accustomed to dignified concert gowns, like those which Pittsburgh matrons (in those days!) wore at their daughter's coming-out teas.

Kitty's gown that evening was really quite outrageous
—the repartée of a conscienceless Parisian designer who
took her hint that she wished something that would be entirely novel in the States. Today, after we have all of us,
even in the uttermost provinces, been educated by Bakst
and the various Ballets Russes, we would accept such a
gown without distrust; but then it was a little disconcerting,
even to the well-disposed. It was constructed of a yard or
two of green velvet—a reviling, shrieking green which would
have made a fright of any woman who had not inextinguish-
able beauty—and it was made without armholes, a device
to which we were then so unaccustomed that it was nothing
less than alarming. The velvet skirt split back from a trans-
parent gold-lace petticoat, gold stockings, gold slippers. The
narrow train was, apparently, looped to both ankles, and
it kept curling about her feet like a serpent's tail, turning
up its gold lining as if it were squirming over on its back.
It was not, we felt, a costume in which to sing Mozart and
Handel and Beethoven.

Kitty sensed the chill in the air, and it amused her. She
liked to be thought a brilliant artist by other artists, but
by the world at large she liked to be thought a daring creature. She had every reason to believe, from experience and
from example, that to shock the great crowd was the surest
way to get its money and to make her name a household
word. Nobody ever became a household word of being an
artist, surely; and you were not a thoroughly paying proposition until your name meant something on the sidewalk and
in the barber-shop. Kitty studied her audience with an appraising eye. She liked the stimulus of this disapprobation.
As she faced this hard-shelled public she felt keen and interested; she knew that she would give such a recital as

cannot often be heard for money. She nodded gaily to the young man at the piano, fell into an attitude of seriousness, and began the group of Beethoven and Mozart songs.

Though McKann would not have admitted it, there were really a great many people in the concert-hall who knew what the prodigal daughter of their country was singing, and how well she was doing it. They thawed gradually under the beauty of her voice and the subtlety of her interpretation. She had sung seldom in concert then, and they had supposed her very dependent upon the accessories of the opera. Clean singing, finished artistry, were not what they expected from her. They began to feel, even, the wayward charm of her personality.

McKann, who stared coldly up at the balconies during her first song, during the second glanced cautiously at the green apparition before him. He was vexed with her for having retained a débutante figure. He comfortably classed all singers—especially operatic singers—as "fat Dutchwomen" or "shifty Sadies," and Kitty would not fit into his clever generalization. She displayed, under his nose, the only kind of figure he considered worth looking at—that of a very young girl, supple and sinuous and quick-silverish; thin, eager shoulders, polished white arms that were nowhere too fat and nowhere too thin. McKann found it agreeable to look at Kitty, but when he saw that the authoritative Mrs. Post, red as a turkey-cock with opinions she was bursting to impart, was studying and appraising the singer through her lorgnette, he gazed indifferently out into the house again. He felt for his watch, but his wife touched him warningly with her elbow—which, he noticed, was not at all like Kitty's.

When Miss Ayrshire finished her first group of songs,

her audience expressed its approval positively, but guard-edly. She smiled bewitchingly upon the people in front, glanced up at the balconies, and then turned to the company huddled on the stage behind her. After her gay and careless bows, she retreated toward the stage door. As she passed McKann, she again brushed lightly against him, and this time she paused long enough to glance down at him and murmur, "Pardon!"

In the moment her bright, curious eyes rested upon him, McKann seemed to see himself as if she were holding a mirror up before him. He beheld himself a heavy, solid figure, unsuitably clad for the time and place, with a florid, square face, well-visored with good living and sane opinions—and inexpressive countenance. Not a rock face, exactly, but a kind of pressed-brick-and-cement face, a "business" face upon which years and feelings had made no mark—in which cocktails might eventually blast out a few hollows. He had never seen himself so distinctly in his shaving-glass as he did in that instant when Kitty Ayrshire's liquid eye held him, when her bright, inquiring glance roamed over his person. After her prehensile train curled over his boot and she was gone, his wife turned to him and said in the tone of approbation one uses when an infant manifests its groping intelligence, "Very gracious of her, I'm sure!" Mrs. Post nodded oracularly. McKann grunted.

Kitty began her second number, a group of romantic German songs which were altogether more her affair than her first number. When she turned once to acknowledge the applause behind her, she caught McKann in the act of yawning behind his hand—he of course wore no gloves —and he thought she frowned a little. This did not embarrass him; it somehow made him feel important. When she retired after the second part of the program, she again looked him over curiously as she passed, and she took marked precaution that her dress did not touch him. Mrs. Post and his wife again commented upon her consideration.

The final number was made up of modern French songs which Kitty sang enchantingly, and at last her frigid public was thoroughly aroused. While she was coming back again and again to smile and curtsy, McKann whispered to his wife that if there were to be encores he had better make a dash for his train.

"Not at all," put in Mrs. Post. "Kitty is going on the same train. She sings in *Faust* at the opera tomorrow night, so she'll take no chances."

McKann once more told himself how sorry he felt for Post. At last Miss Ayrshire returned, escorted by her accompanist, and gave the people what she of course knew they wanted: the most popular aria from the French opera of which the title-rôle had become synonymous with her name—an opera written for her and to her and round about her, by the veteran French composer who adored her, —the last and not the palest flash of his creative fire. This brought her audience all the way. They clamoured for more of it, but she was not to be coerced. She had been unyielding through storms to which this was a summer breeze. She came on once more, shrugged her shoulders, blew them a kiss, and was gone. Her last smile was for that uncomfortable part of her audience seated behind her, and she looked with recognition at McKann and his ladies as she nodded good night to the wooden chairs.

McKann hurried his charges into the foyer by the nearest exit and put them into his motor. Then he went over to the Schenley to have a glass of beer and a rarebit before train-time. He had not, he admitted to himself, been so

much bored as he pretended. The minx herself was well
enough, but it was absurd in his fellow-townsmen to look
owlish and uplifted about her. He had no rooted dislike for
pretty women; he even didn't deny that gay girls had their
places in the world, but they ought to be kept in their place.
He was born a Presbyterian, just as he was born a McKann.
He sat in his pew in the First Church every Sunday, and
he never missed a presbytery meeting when he was in town.
His religion was not very spiritual, certainly, but it was
substantial and concrete, made up of good, hard convictions
and opinions. It had something to do with citizenship, with
whom one ought to marry, with the coal business (in which
his own name was powerful), with the Republican party,
and with all majorities and established precedents. He was
hostile to fads, to enthusiasms, to individualism, to all
changes except in mining machinery and in methods of
transportation.

His equanimity restored by his lunch at the Schenley,
McKann lit a big cigar, got into his taxi, and bowled off
through the sleet.

There was not a sound to be heard or a light to be seen.
The ice glittered on the pavement and on the naked trees.
No restless feet were abroad. At eleven o'clock the rows
of small, comfortable houses looked as empty of the trouble-
some bubble of life as the Allegheny cemetery itself. Suddenly the cab stopped, and McKann thrust his head out of
the window. A woman was standing in the middle of the
street addressing his driver in a tone of excitement. Over
against the curb a lone electric stood despondent in the
storm. The young woman, her cloak blowing about her
turned from the driver to McKann himself, speaking rapidly
and somewhat incoherently.

"Could you not be so kind as to help us? It is Mees

Ayrshire, the singer. The juice is gone out and we cannot
move. We must get to the station. Mademoiselle cannot
miss the train; she sings tomorrow night in New York.
It is very important. Could you not take us to the station
at East Liberty?"

McKann opened the door. "That's all right, but you'll
have to hurry. It's eleven-ten now. You've only got fifteen
minutes to make the train. Tell her to come along."

The maid drew back and looked up at him in amazement.
"But, the hand-luggage to carry, and Mademoiselle to walk!
The street is like glass!"

McKann threw away his cigar and followed her. He stood
silent by the door of the derelict, while the maid explained
that she had found help. The driver had gone off somewhere
to telephone for a car. Miss Ayrshire seemed not at all
apprehensive; she had not doubted that a rescuer would be
forthcoming. She moved deliberately; out of a whirl of skirts
she thrust one fur-topped shoe—McKann saw the flash of
the gold stocking above it—and alighted.

"So kind of you! So fortunate for us!" she murmured.
One hand she placed upon his sleeve, and in the other she
carried an armful of roses that had been sent up to the
concert stage. The petals showered upon the sooty, sleety
pavement as she picked her way along. They would be
lying there tomorrow morning, and the children in those
houses would wonder if there had been a funeral. The maid
followed with two leather bags. As soon as he had lifted
Kitty into his cab she exclaimed:

"My jewel-case! I have forgotten it. It is on the back seat,
please. I am so careless!"

He dashed back, ran his hand along the cushions, and
discovered a small leather bag. When he returned he found

the maid and the luggage bestowed on the front seat, and a place left for him on the back seat beside Kitty and her flowers.

"Shall we be taking you far out of your way?" she asked sweetly. "I haven't an idea where the station is. I'm not even sure about the name. Céline thinks it is East Liberty, but I think it is West Liberty. An odd name, anyway. It is a Bohemian quarter, perhaps? A district where the law relaxes a trifle?"

McKann replied grimly that he didn't think the name referred to that kind of liberty.

"So much the better," sighed Kitty. "I am a Californian; that's the only part of America I know very well, and out there, when we called a place Liberty Hill or Liberty Hollow—well, we meant it. You will excuse me if I'm uncommunicative, won't you? I must not talk in the raw air. My throat is sensitive after a long program." She lay back in her corner and closed her eyes.

When the cab rolled down the incline at East Liberty station, the New York express was whistling in. A porter opened the door. McKann sprang out, gave him a claim check and his Pullman ticket, and told him to get his bag at the check-stand and rush it on that train.

Miss Ayrshire, having gathered up her flowers, put out her hand to take his arm. "Why, it's you!" she exclaimed, as she saw his face in the light. "What a coincidence!" She made no further move to alight, but sat smiling as if she had just seated herself in a drawing-room and were ready for talk and a cup of tea.

McKann caught her arm. "You must hurry, Miss Ayrshire, if you mean to catch that train. It stops here only a moment. Can you run?"

"Can I run!" she laughed. "Try me!"

As they raced through the tunnel and up the inside stair-way, McKann admitted that he had never before made a dash with feet so quick and sure stepping out beside him. The white-furred boots chased each other like lambs at play, the gold stockings flashed like the spokes of a bicycle wheel in the sun. They reached the door of Miss Ayrshire's state-room just as the train began to pull out. McKann was ashamed of the way he was panting, for Kitty's breathing was as soft and regular as when she was reclining on the back seat of his taxi. It had somehow run in his head that all these stage women were in a poor lot physically—unsound, overfed creatures, like canaries that are kept in a cage and stuffed with song-restorer. He retreated to escape her thanks. "Good night! Pleasant journey! Pleasant dreams!" With a friendly nod in Kitty's direction he closed the door behind him.

He was somewhat surprised to find his own bag, his Pullman ticket in the strap, on the seat just outside Kitty's door. But there was nothing strange about it. He had got the last section left on the train, No. 13, next the drawing-room. Every other berth in the car was made up. He was just starting to look for the porter when the door of the state-room opened and Kitty Ayrshire came out. She seated her-self carelessly in the front seat beside his bag.

"Please talk to me a little," she said coaxingly. "I'm always wakeful after I sing, and I have to hunt some one to talk to. Céline and I get so tired of each other. We can speak very low, and we shall not disturb any one." She crossed her feet and rested her elbow on his Gladstone. Though she still wore her gold slippers and stockings, she did not, he thanked Heaven, have on her concert gown, but a very demure black velvet with some sort of pearl trimming about the neck. "Wasn't it funny," she proceeded, "that it happened to be you who picked me up? I wanted a word with you anyway."

McKann smiled in a way that meant he wasn't being taken in. "Did you? We are not very old acquaintances."

"No, perhaps not. But you disapproved tonight, and I thought I was singing very well. You are very critical in such matters?"

He had been standing, but now he sat down. "My dear young lady, I am not critical at all. I know nothing about 'such matters.' "

"And care less?" she said for him. "Well, then we know where we are, in so far as that is concerned. What did displease you? My gown, perhaps? It may seem a little *outré* here, but it's the sort of thing all the imaginative designers abroad are doing. You like the English sort of concert gown better?"

"About gowns," said McKann, "I know even less than about music. If I looked uncomfortable, it was probably because I was uncomfortable. The seats were bad and the lights were annoying."

Kitty looked up with solicitude. "I was sorry they sold those seats. I don't like to make people uncomfortable in any way. Did the lights give you a headache? They are very trying. They burn one's eyes out in the end, I believe." She paused and waved the porter away with a smile as he came toward them. Half-clad Pittsburghers were tramping up and down the aisle, casting sidelong glances at McKann and his companion. "How much better they look with all their clothes on," she murmured. Then, turning directly to Mc-Kann again: "I saw you were not well seated, but I felt something quite hostile and personal. You were displeased with me. Doubtless many people are, but I seldom get an opportunity to question them. It would be nice if you took the trouble to tell me why you were displeased."

She spoke frankly, pleasantly, without a shadow of challenge or hauteur. She did not seem to be angling for compliments. McKann settled himself in his seat. He thought he would try her out. She had come for it, and he would let her have it. He found, however, that it was harder to formulate the grounds of his disapproval than he would have supposed. Now that he sat face to face with her, now that she was leaning against his bag, he had no wish to hurt her.

"I'm a hard-headed businessman," he said evasively, "and I don't much believe in any of you fluffy-ruffles people. I have a sort of natural distrust of them all, the men more than the women."

She looked thoughtful. "Artists, you mean?" drawing her words slowly. "What is your business?"

"Coal."

"I don't feel any natural distrust of businessmen, and I know ever so many. I don't know any coal-men, but I think I could become very much interested in coal. Am I larger-minded than you?"

McKann laughed. "I don't think you know when you are interested or when you are not. I don't believe you know what it feels like to be really interested. There is so much fake about your profession. It's an affectation on both sides. I know a great many of the people who went to hear you tonight, and I know that most of them neither know nor care anything about music. They imagine they do, because it's supposed to be the proper thing."

Kitty sat upright and looked interested. She was certainly
a lovely creature—the only one of her tribe he had ever
seen that he would cross the street to see again. Those were
remarkable eyes she had—curious, penetrating, restless,
somehow imprudent, but not at all dulled by self-conceit.

"But isn't that so in everything?" she cried. "How many
of your clerks are honest because of a fine, individual sense
of honour? They are honest because it is the accepted rule
of good conduct in business. Do you know"—she looked at
him squarely—"I thought you would have something quite
definite to say to me; but this is funny-paper stuff, the sort
of objection I'd expect from your office-boy."

"Then you don't think it silly for a lot of people to get
together and pretend to enjoy something they know nothing
about?"

"Of course I think it silly, but that's the way God made
audiences. Don't people go to church in exactly the same
way? If there were a spiritual-pressure test-machine at the
door, I suspect not many of you would get to your pews."

"How do you know I go to church?"

She shrugged her shoulders. "Oh, people with these old,
ready-made opinions usually go to church. But you can't
evade me like that." She tapped the edge of his seat
with the toe of her gold slipper. "You sat there all evening,
glaring at me as if you could eat me alive. Now I give you a
chance to state your objections, and you merely criticize my
audience. What is it? Is it merely that you happen to dislike my personality? In that case, of course, I won't press
you."

"No," McKann frowned, "I perhaps dislike your professional personality. As I told you, I have a natural distrust
of your variety."

"Natural, I wonder?" Kitty murmured. "I don't see why you should naturally dislike singers any more than I naturally dislike coal-men. I don't classify people by their occupations. Doubtless I should find some coal-men repulsive and you may find some singers so. But I have reason to believe that, at least, I'm one of the less repellent."

"I don't doubt it," McKann laughed, "and you're a shrewd woman to boot. But you are, all of you, according to my standards, light people. You're brilliant, some of you, but you've no depth."

Kitty seemed to assent, with a dive of her girlish head. "Well, it's a merit in some things to be heavy, and in others to be light. Some things are meant to go deep, and others to go high. Do you want all the women in the world to be profound?"

"You are all," he went on steadily, watching her with indulgence, "fed on hectic emotions. You are pampered. You don't help to carry the burdens of the world. You are self-indulgent and appetent."

"Yes, I am," she assented, with a candour which he did not expect. "Not all artists are, but I am. Why not? If I could once get a convincing statement as to why I should not be self-indulgent, I might change my ways. As for the burdens of the world—" Kitty rested her chin on her clasped hands and looked thoughtful. "One should give pleasure to others. My dear sir, granting that the great majority of people can't enjoy anything very keenly, you'll admit that I give pleasure to many more people than you do. One should help others who are less fortunate; at present I am supporting just eight people, besides those I hire. There was never another family in California that had so many cripples and hard-luckers as that into which I had the honour to

be born. The only ones who could take care of themselves
were ruined by the San Francisco earthquake some time
ago. One should make personal sacrifices. I do; I give money
and time and effort to talented students. Oh, I give something much more than that! something that you probably
have never given to any one. I give, to the really gifted ones,
my *wish*, my desire, my light, if I have any; and that, Mr.
Worldly Wiseman, is like giving one's blood! It's the kind of
thing you prudent people never give. That is what was in
the box of precious ointment." Kitty threw off her fervour
with a slight gesture, as if it were a scarf, and leaned back,
tucking her slipper up on the edge of his seat. "If you saw
the houses I keep up," she sighed, "and the people I employ,
and the motor-cars I run— And, after all, I've only this
to do it with." She indicated her slendor person, which
Marshall could almost have broken in two with his bare
hands.

She was, he thought, very much like any other charming
woman, except that she was more so. Her familiarity was
natural and simple. She was at ease because she was not
afraid of him or of herself, or of certain half-clad acquaintances of his who had been wandering up and down the car
oftener than was necessary. Well, he was not afraid, either.

Kitty put her arms over her head and sighed again, feeling
the smooth part in her black hair. Her head was small—
capable of great agitation, like a bird's; or of great resigna-
tion, like a nun's. "I can't see why I shouldn't be self-
indulgent, when I indulge others. I can't understand your
equivocal scheme of ethics. Now I can understand Count
Tolstoy's, perfectly. I had a long talk with him once, about
his book 'What is Art?' As nearly as I could get it, he
believes that we are a race who can exist only by gratifying

appetites; the appetites are evil, and the existence they carry on is evil. We were always sad, he says, without knowing why; even in the Stone Age. In some miraculous way a divine ideal was disclosed to us, directly at variance with our appetites. It gave us a new craving, which we could only satisfy by starving all the other hungers in us. Happiness lies in ceasing to be and to cause being, because the thing revealed to us is dearer than any existence our appetites can ever get for us. I can understand that. It's something one often feels in art. It is even the subject of the greatest of all operas, which, because I can never hope to sing it, I love more than all the others." Kitty pulled herself up. "Perhaps you agree with Tolstoy?" she added languidly.

"No; I think he's a crank," said McKann, cheerfully.

"What do you mean by a crank?"

"I mean an extremist."

Kitty laughed. "Weighty word! You'll always have a world full of people who keep to the golden mean. Why bother yourself about me and Tolstoy?"

"I don't, except when you bother me."

"Poor man! It's true this isn't your fault. Still, you did provoke it by glaring at me. Why did you go to the concert?"

"I was dragged."

"I might have known!" she chuckled, and shook her head. "No, you don't give me any good reasons. Your morality seems to me the compromise of cowardice, apologetic and sneaking. When righteousness becomes alive and burning, you hate it as much as you do beauty. You want a little of each in your life, perhaps—adulterated, sterilized, with the sting taken out. It's true enough they are both fearsome things when they get loose in the world; they don't, often."

McKann hated tall talk. "My views on women," he said slowly, "are simple."

"Doubtless," Kitty responded dryly, "but are they consistent? Do you apply them to your stenographers as well as to me? I take it for granted you have unmarried stenographers. Their position, economically, is the same as mine."

McKann studied the toe of her shoe. "With a woman, everything comes back to one thing." His manner was judicial.

She laughed indulgently. "So we are getting down to brass tacks, eh? I have beaten you in argument, and now you are leading trumps." She put her hands behind her head and her lips parted in a half-yawn. "Does everything come back to one thing? I wish I knew! It's more than likely that, under the same conditions, I should have been very like your stenographers—if they are good ones. Whatever I was, I would have been a good one. I think people are very much alike. You are more different than any one I have met for some time, but I know that there are a great many more at home like you. And even you—I believe there is a real creature down under these custom-made prejudices that save you the trouble of thinking. If you and I were shipwrecked on a desert island, I have no doubt that we would come to a simple and natural understanding. I'm neither a coward nor a shirk. You would find, if you had to undertake any enterprise of danger or difficulty with a woman, that there are several qualifications quite as important as the one to which you doubtless refer."

McKann felt nervously for his watch-chain. "Of course," he brought out, "I am not laying down any generalizations —" His brows wrinkled.

"Oh, aren't you?" murmured Kitty. "Then I totally

misunderstood. But remember"—holding up a finger—"it
is you, not I, who are afraid to pursue this subject further.
Now, I'll tell you something." She leaned forward and
clasped her slim, white hands about her velvet knee. "I am
as much a victim of these ineradicable prejudices as you.
Your stenographer seems to you a better sort. Well, she
does to me. Just because her life is, presumably, greyer than
mine, she seems better. My mind tells me that dullness, and
a mediocre order of ability, and poverty, are not in themselves admirable things. Yet in my heart I always feel that
the sales-women in shops and the working girls in factories
are more meritorious than I. Many of them, with my opportunities, would be more selfish than I am. Some of them,
with their own opportunities, are more selfish. Yet I make
this sentimental genuflection before the nun and the char-
woman. Tell me, haven't you any weakness? Isn't there any
foolish natural thing that unbends you a trifle and makes
you feel gay?"

"I like to go fishing."

"To see how many fish you can catch?"

"No, I like the woods and the weather. I like to play
a fish and work hard for him. I like the pussy-willows and
the cold; and the sky, whether it's blue or grey—night
coming on, everything about it."

He spoke devoutly, and Kitty watched him through half-
closed eyes. "And you like to feel that there are light-minded
girls like me, who only care about the inside of shops and
theatres and hotels, eh? You amuse me, you and your fish!
But I mustn't keep you any longer. Haven't I given you
every opportunity to state your case against me? I thought
you would have more to say for yourself. Do you know, I
believe it's not a case you have at all, but a grudge. I believe

you are envious, that you'd like to be a tenor, and a perfect
lady-killer!" She rose, smiling, and paused with her hand on
the door of her state-room. "Anyhow, thank you for a
pleasant evening. And, by the way, dream of me tonight,
and not of either of those ladies who sat beside you. It does
not matter much whom we live with in this world, but it
matters a great deal whom we dream of." She noticed his
bricky flush. "You are very naïf, after all, but, oh, so cau-
tious! You are naturally afraid of everything new, just as I
naturally want to try everything: new people, new religions
—new miseries, even. If only there were more new things—
If only you were really new! I might learn something. I'm
like the Queen of Sheba—I'm not above learning. But you,
my friend, would be afraid to try a new shaving soap. It isn't
gravitation that holds the world in place; it's the lazy, obese
cowardice of the people on it. All the same"—taking his
hand and smiling encouragingly—"I'm going to haunt you
a little. *Adios!*"

When Kitty entered her state-room, Céline, in her dress-
ing-gown, was nodding by the window.

"Mademoiselle found the fat gentleman interesting?" she
asked. "It is nearly one."

"Negatively interesting. His kind always say the same
thing. If I could find one really intelligent man who held his
views, I should adopt them."

"Monsieur did not look like an original," murmured
Céline, as she began to take down her lady's hair.

McKann slept heavily, as usual, and the porter had to
shake him in the morning. He sat up in his berth, and, after
composing his hair with his fingers, began to hunt about for
his clothes. As he put up the window-blind some bright object

in the little hammock over his bed caught the sunlight and glittered. He stared and picked up a delicately turned gold slipper.

"Minx! hussy!" he ejaculated. "All that tall talk—! Probably got it from some man who hangs about; learned it off like a parrot. Did she poke this in here herself last night, or did she send that sneak-faced Frenchwoman? I like her nerve!" He wondered whether he might have been breathing audibly when the intruder thrust her head between his curtains. He was conscious that he did not look a Prince Charming in his sleep. He dressed as fast as he could, and, when he was ready to go to the washroom, glared at the slipper. If the porter should start to make up his berth in his absence—He caught the slipper, wrapped it in his pajama jacket, and thrust it into his bag. He escaped from the train without seeing his tormentor again.

Later McKann threw the slipper into the wastebasket in his room at the Knickerbocker, but the chambermaid, seeing that it was new and mateless, thought there must be a mistake, and placed it in his clothes-closet. He found it there when he returned from the theatre that evening. Considerably mellowed by food and drink and cheerful company, he took the slipper in his hand and decided to keep it as a reminder that absurd things could happen to people of the most clocklike deportment. When he got back to Pittsburgh, he stuck it in a lock-box in his vault, safe from prying clerks.

McKann has been ill for five years now, poor fellow! He still goes to the office, because it is the only place that interests him, but his partners do most of the work, and his clerks find him sadly changed—"morbid," they call his state of mind. He has had the pine-trees in his yard cut down because they remind him of cemeteries. On Sundays or holidays, when the office is empty, and he takes his will or his insurance-policies out of his lock-box, he often puts the tarnished gold slipper on his desk and looks at it. Somehow it suggests life to his tired mind, as his pine-trees suggested death—life and youth. When he drops over some day, his executors will be puzzled by the slipper.

As for Kitty Ayrshire, she has played so many jokes, practical and impractical, since then, that she has long ago forgotten the night when she threw away a slipper to be a thorn in the side of a just man.

BIOGRAPHIES

WILLA CATHER (1876–1947) was born in Virginia. One of her major themes was the courage and strength of the settlers of the frontier. *One of Ours,* one of her novels that dealt with this theme, won the Pulitzer Prize in 1922. Some of her best-known books are *O, Pioneers!* (1913), *My Antonia* (1918), and *Death Comes for the Archbishop* (1927).

ALICE CHILDRESS was born in 1920 in Charleston, South Carolina. She has been an actress and director of the American Negro Theatre in New York City, where she now lives. She is the author of *A Hero Ain't Nothin' But a Sandwich,* a novel published in 1973.

O. HENRY (1862–1910) was a pseudonym for William Sydney Porter, a native of Greensboro, North Carolina. In 1898, a shortage in the Texas bank in which O. Henry was working was attributed to him and he served three years in jail, where he started writing short stories. After his release from jail, O. Henry settled in New York City, where he spent the remainder of his lifetime writing about 300 stories, collected in *Cabbages and Kings* (1904), *Heart of the West* (1907), and numerous other volumes.

HENRY JAMES (1843–1916), born in New York City, wrote numerous short stories and novels, including *The American, The Portrait of a Lady,* and *Daisy Miller.* He traveled widely and in 1876 settled in London, becoming a British citizen in 1915.

SARAH ORNE JEWETT (1849–1909) was born in Maine. As a young girl she went with her father, a doctor, on his rounds, becoming familiar with the countryside and its people. These experiences formed the basis for her stories of New England life, published in *Tales of New England* (1890), *The Country of the Pointed Firs* (1896), and other books.

MARGARET LAURENCE, born in Canada in 1926, started to write when she was eight years old. She lived in Somaliland and Ghana for a number of years with her husband, a civil engineer, and much of her writing, both stories and novels, is about Africa. She now lives in London with her family.

KATHERINE MANSFIELD (1888–1923) was born in New Zealand, though most of her short life was spent in Europe. She is regarded as a master of the short story.

ALICE MUNRO was born in 1931 in Ontario, Canada. Her first collection of short stories, *Dance of the Happy Shades*, earned her the Governor General's Award. She has also written a novel, *Lives of Girls and Women*.

JEAN RHYS was born in 1894 in England. With the advent of a strong feminist movement in the 1970s, many of her early short stories and novels were rediscovered. Her novels include *After Leaving Mr. MacKenzie* and *Good Morning, Midnight*.

JEAN WHEELER SMITH was born in Detroit in 1942. She has been
    active in the civil rights movement in the South and
    has been involved in the problems of urban food pro-
    duction. She is the author of several other short stories
    and many scientific articles.

G. B. (GLADYS BRONWYN) STERN (1891–1973) was born in Lon-
    don. She was a novelist, dramatist, journalist and short
    story writer.

ARTHUR SYMONS (1865–1945) was born in Milford Haven, En-
    gland. He is known mostly as a poet and critic; his best-
    known critical work is *The Symbolist Movement in
    Literature*. Symons was editor of *The Savoy* until he
    went through a period of insanity from 1908 to 1910,
    which he wrote about in his *Confessions* in 1930.

17994

SC
Wor   The World outside

DATE			
Reserve			